# MOSEY

# MOSEY

## The Remarkable Friendship of a Boy and His Elephant

### RALPH HELFER

ORCHARD  ★  NEW YORK

*An Imprint of Scholastic Inc.*

ACKNOWLEDGMENTS

As we travel through life, we occasionally meet someone whose creative thinking is linked to our own. It's quite important to hold on tightly and cement the connection to foster mutual growth and creativity. I have been fortunate to find such a person. Rebecca St. George has been my inspiration and guide throughout the writing of this book. I could not have done it without her.

I would also like to thank Ellen Dreyer of Orchard Books, whose editing skills and patience helped make *Mosey* a reality. Her tireless hours and many suggestions were greatly appreciated.

Copyright © 2002 by Ralph Helfer

Library of Congress Cataloging-in-Publication Data
Helfer, Ralph.
Mosey : the remarkable friendship of a boy and his elephant /
by Ralph Helfer. — lst ed.
p.   cm.
Based on the author's Modoc.
Summary: Tells the true story of a boy's devotion to a beloved circus elephant
and the ordeals they endured to stay together.
ISBN 0-439-29313-8
1. Modoc (Elephant) — Juvenile literature.   2. Circus animals — Juvenile literature.
3. Human-animal relationships — Juvenile literature.   4. Gunterstein, Bram —
Childhood and youth—Juvenile literature.   [1. Modoc (Elephant).
2. Gunterstein, Bram — Childhood and youth.   3. Circus animals.   4. Human-
animal relationships.]   I. Helfer, Ralph. Modoc.   II. Title.
GV1831.E4   H47   2002   791.3'2'0929—dc21   2001032933

10 9 8 7 6 5 4 3 2 1     02 03 04 05
The text type was set in 11.5-point Galliard.
Printed in U.S.A.
First edition, May 2002

THIS BOOK
IS DEDICATED TO
TIVA, RIAN AND SAVANAH

# AUTHOR'S NOTE

It took me many years to write *Mosey.* I had to allow myself the time to relive the pain and sorrow, as well as all of the wonderful times we spent together. Although I owned Mosey for twenty years, I had to research her life before we found each other.

She was a magnificent elephant. As you read, you will discover that Mosey and Bram, the boy she loved more than anything else, shared a special, almost intangible link.

Bram and Mosey had been born on the same day, on Bram's family's farm in Germany. They grew up together in the circus, and shared many adventures — both exciting and dangerous — from Germany to India and finally to the United States. Then they were separated for many years, and finally, after Bram's tireless efforts, they were reunited on my California ranch.

Bram told me much of Mosey's story. I also learned about her from newspaper and magazine articles; from circus people, usually animal trainers; and even from people who saw her perform.

I have spent my entire life with exotic animals — lions, tigers, elephants, hundreds of different species — but in all that time, only a handful had the gift that Mosey had. There was something uncanny about her that made people feel as if she could look within them, understanding their deepest thoughts and feelings.

I took all the information I gathered and allowed my imagination to fill in the missing pieces — the dialogue, action, and so on — that could not be documented or proven. In this way I came up with a story as true as I could make it.

Maybe you, too, have had the privilege of knowing a Mosey, some animal with the gift of understanding humans. Whether you have or not, please share my adventure. I hope you will come to love and cherish the memory of Mosey as much as I do.

This book was written for all the animal lovers of the world but most of all it was written in memory of the
"World's Greatest Elephant,"
Mosey.

# MOSEY

 **ONE**

The old barn door creaked open, admitting a shaft of morning light that spilled across the floor and onto the thirteen-year-old boy curled up in a deep pile of straw. The trunk of an elephant was wrapped around him.

"Wake up, you two!" Josef called from the doorway.

Bram smiled as he opened his eyes, squinting against the bright, late August sun. Suddenly he remembered that today was Saturday — circus day! He had to help Mosey get ready for her weekend performance.

"Morning, Papa!" Bram said, yawning and stretching the nighttime kinks out of his arms and legs. He encircled Mosey's trunk and hugged it gently.

"Come on, Mosey. You sure are a sound sleeper!"

Mosey opened one eye and gazed at him. Her belly rumbled with affection as she tousled his straight brown hair with the end of her trunk.

What a glorious feeling — to awaken with an elephant. Bram picked up a long piece of straw and tickled way up inside of her trunk. The sneeze blew away all the straw around him. Bram chuckled. "Enough of this now. Come on, we have to eat, then there's work to be done."

Mosey stood up, shook her huge frame free of most of the straw, and, with her trunk, blew the rest off while Bram went to get her breakfast.

Feeding an elephant was no small matter. Bram was about to load a bale of hay into the wheelbarrow when, suddenly, someone came up from behind and covered his eyes. He lost his grip, and the wheelbarrow toppled over. "Gertie!" he exclaimed, spinning around to face a lanky, blond, brown-eyed girl.

"I'm not here to see you. I came to see Mosey," she said, grinning.

Bram smiled, his heart beating rapidly. He didn't want to admit that she'd made him jump. "Are you coming to the circus?"

She shook her head, her silky hair flowing from side to side. "Mama wants me to stay home and help with the chores."

"Oh." He heard the disappointment in his voice as he replied, "You want to help me feed her?"

"Sure."

Gertie grabbed the bucket and scooped out a gallon of grain consisting of barley, oats, and molasses, while Bram righted the wheelbarrow and loaded the bale of hay. He set half at Mosey's feet. Gertie poured the grain in a small pile next to the hay. Then they cut up a few apples and oranges as a special treat.

The rest of Mosey's food would be loaded in the truck for her lunch at the circus. Mosey couldn't eat too much before a performance. She might get a stomachache, and for an elephant, that could be a big problem.

But afterward she would have a banquet! Two dozen apples, a dozen oranges, twelve loaves of bread, two bunches of carrots, and several pounds of potatoes.

Bram patted Mosey as she got down to the business of eating. Feeling around with her trunk, she chose some grain, then scooped it up with the tip of her trunk and placed it deep in her mouth where her molars could grind it. She had to chew for a long time before the food was small enough to swallow. Then, with the help of her front toes, she pressed some hay into the curve of her trunk and put it into her mouth. She was very neat, picking up any food that fell to the ground and adding it to the piles.

After watching Mosey for a few minutes, Gertie walked with Bram to the house and, with a quick hug, went on her way. Blushing, Bram watched her go, then went inside.

"Morning, Mama." He paused by the stove to give his mother a peck on the cheek. "Gertie and I just fed Mosey, she'll be ready to go." He joined Josef at the table.

Katrina, Bram's mother, was an intelligent, hardworking woman who was born in Norway. Heavyset, she wore her long blond hair tied neatly in a bun and radiated a natural beauty. She always believed that "the first meal was the best meal" and now set out a delicious-smelling platter of potato pancakes smothered in honey and a bowl of raspberries from the garden. Then she brought Bram a large glass of milk, fresh from their cow. Josef was already sipping the strong coffee he favored.

Bram ate quickly, thanked his mother, and, seeing his friend Curpo outside, bolted out the door. "Hey, Curpo, wait!" he cried. The moment he caught up, Curpo handed him a scrub brush. "Oh, no," Bram said, smiling, "it's your turn. I'll handle the hose."

"Yer a bit on the sassy side this morning, mate," Curpo joked. "Okay, let's get it done!"

Curpo was a dwarf, but he didn't like being called that. He preferred "small person." Even though he was only four feet tall, he was quite strong. He sported a rather prominent chin and a distinctive hump on his back. He was constantly getting his shirt hung up on it and needed Bram's help to pull it off. Leather shorts, high-top boots, and a gold medallion hanging from a chain around his neck completed his attire.

Curpo had come to Germany from England eight years before, in 1909, looking for a job in the circus. The Wunderzircus, a small circus on the edge of the Black Forest for which Bram's father worked, wanted to hire him as "the world's smallest dwarf," and they were going to call him "Humps." It was just too humiliating. Bram convinced his father to hire Curpo as a keeper, even though Josef was afraid that Mosey might accidentally step on him. But his concern was unfounded.

Bram and Curpo spent the next two hours scrubbing and cleaning both Mosey and the truck. First Curpo lay Mosey down on the grass outside the barn to give her a bath. Bram turned on the garden hose while Curpo scrambled up her head and onto her back. As Bram sprayed, Curpo brushed her down with a strong scrub brush. Bram teasingly let the spray drift a little, hitting Curpo with it.

"Bram!" he yelled, turning his back to avoid the spray. "Ay, mate, yer in fer it now! Wait'll I get ya!"

They picked, cleaned, and applied hydrogen peroxide

to scratches and insect or chigger bites that might become infected.

Then they cleaned out her ears with a whole bunch of rags, and trimmed her nails with a rasp and clippers. They spread out a fresh supply of straw for her in the truck so she wouldn't slip on the floor.

"You're beautiful, you are," said Curpo when they were through. They loaded her onto the truck, which rocked back and forth with her weight.

"Mosey sure has grown a lot, Papa," exclaimed Bram. "She barely fits."

"Ja, that's for sure, son. When she was born, she weighed only two hundred and twenty-five pounds. By the last count, she weighed in at six thousand."

Curpo helped Bram put the leg chains on. Bram remembered how his father taught him to put them on Mosey when she was quite young. At first he thought it was cruel, but when his father explained to him he understood why the chains were important.

"When elephants get big," his father had said, "they can do just about anything they want to. We humans are too little to control them, so we need help. All exotic animals must be controlled in some way. Most are caged. But elephants are too big for that, so we use a chain. One is put on the front foot and another on the back foot.

Every day they are rotated and put on loose so the elephant's legs won't develop any sores. It's just like wearing a necklace." Josef smiled. "And this way, they can't go around knocking over buildings and things."

Bram once saw Mosey accidentally break her chain and attempt to fix it. She held both pieces up with her trunk and tried to tie a knot. When that didn't work, she put her foot on one end of the broken chain to hold it steady; then, grasping the other end with her trunk, she attempted to tie them together. She got the knot all right, but it slipped out, and she ended up hiding the broken part in the hay. Bram watched from behind the hay pile. It would have hurt her feelings to know he'd seen what happened.

"You know, Curpo, Papa says when he retires I'll become Mosey's trainer."

"I know, I know, Bram. Blimey, yer've told me that a 'undred times," said Curpo, who was under Mosey, fastening her hind leg chain to the floor.

"Well, it's true. Then I'll wear the red-and-gold elephant-trainer costume with the high boots. I could feature you in the act, you know: 'The world's smallest man, with Mosey, the world's largest animal.'" Bram raised his hands above his head as though framing an imaginary sign.

"Yer always were a dreamer, Bram. Come on, give me a 'and with these chains," said Curpo, peeking out between Mosey's legs.

Bram had always wanted to be an elephant trainer like his father. Ever since he was eight years old, he had been allowed to accompany Josef to the circus. He'd help feed, water, and brush Mosey before each show. Now he was her constant companion and assisted his father in her training and performances.

Josef had worked for the Wunderzircus for as long as Bram could remember. He was considered by his peers to be the best elephant trainer in all of Europe. He held the position of head trainer and was in charge of all the animals, but the elephants were his favorites. He used a lot of patience, understanding, and affection in his work, and believed in never abusing the animals.

But in the past year, Josef hadn't been feeling too well. He coughed constantly and didn't have as much energy as in the past. A gray pallor had settled over his gaunt face, and his deep-set eyes seemed almost haunted. Bram thought it was due to his excessive smoking. He begged him to stop, but his father, with a wave of his hand, would say, "Tomorrow, tomorrow." But he never did. "Tomorrow" never came. Bram worried about him constantly.

Mosey belonged to the circus owner, Herr Gobel. When he found out that Emma, one of his elephants, was pregnant, he asked Josef if he could keep her in his barn until the baby was born. Herr Gobel was afraid that a delicate newborn might catch cold staying in a circus tent, especially given how brutal the German winters were.

But that was thirteen years ago. The Gunterstein family had fallen in love with Mosey, and all agreed it would be best for the elephant to stay on. This way, Josef could focus on her training. He had special plans for an act that would feature Mosey and Bram doing a performance that had only been done once before.

As soon as Mosey was secured in the truck, Bram gave her some of his mother's cookies — her favorite treat. Then she wrapped her trunk around Bram and pulled him in close to her. She made a sound that Bram called a "belly rumble" because that's exactly what it was. If he got down really low, he could hear gurgling and rumbling inside Mosey's stomach. That was her way of showing affection. In the truck it echoed and sounded like distant thunder.

Then Josef closed the big rear doors and opened the side windows of the truck to give Mosey plenty of fresh air. Bram helped Curpo into the cab and jumped in. The big motor roared to life, and Mosey answered with an ear-piercing trumpet. Bram glanced in the rearview mirror and smiled to glimpse her trunk sticking out the window, as usual, for all to see. Josef put the truck in gear and headed down the road. It was a beautiful day, and they were off to the circus.

# TWO

As they approached the Wunderzircus grounds a half hour later, Bram saw that the line to the ticket booth already stretched all the way to the road. The oom-pah-pah of the calliope music only seemed to heighten the sense of fun and excitement among the gaily dressed crowd.

Josef opened the back of the truck and carefully backed Mosey out. Then, once Bram and Curpo had brushed her off, they all headed for the main gate. Josef liked to use this entrance instead of the back gate because he knew the children loved to see and pet Mosey. The crowds parted as Mosey and her entourage slowly headed down the fairway.

"Hi, String! How's the weather up there?" said Curpo.

String was the tall man of the circus. He wore candy-striped clothes and a huge top hat that made him appear even taller. Not that that was necessary: At eight feet tall, he towered over everyone. He was also the official greeter, standing at the entrance to the fairgrounds.

Tipping his tall striped hat, he smiled. "How ya do-ing, Bram? Hi, Curpo. Good morning, Mr. Gunterstein." Then to Mosey, "I've got something special for you, lady."

He reached over and gave her a big juicy apple. She crunched it in two, some of the juice running down her cheeks. Then she blasted a "thank you" as they contin-ued down the midway.

The midway was aswirl with smells, sounds, and col-ors. The vivid reds and golds of the circus tents sparkled in the sun, animals paced nervously in their cages, and the delicious aroma of popping popcorn wafted through the air. Children got their faces stuck to fluffy cotton candy, and steaming sausages were served up, dripping with sauerkraut, mustard, and pickles.

On one side of the midway were the sideshows. The barkers called through megaphones, hailing the crowd and tempting them to come and see their unusual acts.

"Step right up and see Bolt, the Electric Man! Watch as lightning flashes from one hand to the other!"

"Mr. Twist — he can tie himself in knots!"

"Josephine, the Bearded Lady!"

"Jobo, the man who walks on nails, and Volcano, the fire-eater!"

Bram greeted them with a wave, Mosey trumpeted her hello. This was Bram's family away from home.

The children ran alongside Mosey, patting her sides. Some held her tail and others jumped, trying to reach her ear. Those who couldn't reach, petted her legs, while their parents tried to pull them back, fearing they would be stepped on.

Farther down the midway were the menagerie tents. First came the camels, horses, llamas, and ponies, followed by the bears and chimps, then — set apart in their own area — the beautiful, huge Bengal tigers and African lions, some weighing over four hundred pounds. They were one of the biggest attractions. Finally, at the very end of the midway stood the largest animal tent of all. It housed the "jumbos," which is what circus people call elephants.

At the far end of the circus grounds was a large field where the big tent was erected. This was where the public came to watch the two daily performances. Sometimes, if the crowds were very large, a third show would be held later. Two trailers parked nearby housed the main offices.

Mosey trumpeted her arrival as they arrived at the elephant tent. A loud response from within was heard.

"Bram, I'm going over to the wardrobe trailer. Will you and Curpo put Mosey in the lineup?"

"Okay, Papa," Bram said.

Josef continued, "And don't forget to water and feed everybody, okay?"

"Okay, Papa," Bram answered. Then turning to Mosey, "Move up, girl, get in line with the others."

Mosey ambled into the tent, did a pivot, and backed in alongside the other elephants — Emma, Mosey's mother; Krono, a young bull elephant; and finally Tina, the smallest of them all. The trumpeting was ear shattering, each greeting Mosey, touching her with their trunks and bellowing their happiness to see her. Mosey put the tip of her trunk in Emma's mouth. Bram knew this was a special sign of affection between them.

Curpo connected the water hose and pulled it over to Mosey, then turned on the faucet. Mosey picked up the hose with her trunk and put the nozzle in her mouth. By putting her foot gently on the hose, she could stop or slow down the flow whenever she wished.

Bram and Curpo gathered up the performance blankets and headpieces. To each elephant they gave the command "Head down." Each elephant lowered its head so that the colorful blue-and-gold-sequined headband could be put on and fastened. "Come down," Bram said, and each elephant slowly settled into a sphinxlike position, which allowed the blankets to be draped over them easily. The heavy buckles were fastened underneath to keep the blankets secure while the elephants performed.

Curpo strapped leg brackets with silver bells onto each of their front legs. Tina loved to play with the bells by shaking her legs.

Meanwhile, Bram removed the elephants' leg chains.

Finally, Bram gave the command "Tail up." Emma, being the biggest elephant, moved ahead, followed by Mosey, Krono, and finally Tina, still trying to ring the bells. Each elephant held the tail of the one in front. As Bram gave the command "Move up," Josef entered the tent, decked out in the customary elephant trainer outfit: a silver sequined jacket, black boots, a loose-fitting white tunic, and wide silver belt with blue trousers. Bram looked at his father, proud to be the son of a man who was held in such high esteem as an elephant trainer. He knew someday he, too, would be in the center ring — with Mosey.

Josef began the performance by putting the quartet through a combination of sit-ups, front leg stands, trunk ups, hind leg stands, and a unique dance of skips and pivots keeping in time with the calliope. The performance ended with Josef standing high on Emma's head as all three elephants did a hind leg stand to the cheering crowd.

When they were finished, Bram and Curpo took the elephants back to their tent, congratulating them on a job well done, while Josef changed his costume. While they were removing the elephants' attire and accessories, a roustabout appeared wheeling a cart of hay for Bram to feed to the elephants. He slipped Mosey a half-full bottle of his soda. She was quite adept at holding the bottle with her trunk and guzzling it down in one gulp.

"Don't get too comfortable," he told Bram, who sat on a hay bale watching Mosey drink. "I hear they're gonna sell the circus."

## THREE

"What?" Bram said, sitting bolt upright, his ears stinging at the roustabout's words.

"Old man Gobel's sick. He's selling the circus to the highest bidder."

"How do you know?"

The roustabout leaned against the hay cart, dusted his hands, and shrugged. "Word gets around," he said. Seeing the shocked look on Bram's face, he turned away. "Well, guess I'll be moving on. See ya."

He passed Josef, who was just entering the tent. Bram noticed that his father seemed depressed, but he couldn't help blurting out his question.

"Papa, did you hear about the circus being sold?"

"I know Herr Gobel's quite sick," said Josef, putting a hand on Bram's shoulder. "Maybe he's just thinking about it."

Bram and Curpo loaded Mosey into the truck in silence.

Josef seemed disheartened during the ride home. Katrina met him at the front door and accompanied him up the stairs.

"Don't yer worry, Bram," Curpo told him as they got Mosey settled in the barn, "it's probably just rumors."

Bram wanted to be reassured by Curpo's words, but the uneasy feeling in the pit of his stomach wouldn't go away.

That evening, Bram sat on a hay bale watching Mosey munch hay. The light of a lantern cast tall shadows on the barn walls. He looked up as his father came in, carrying a cloth bundle. Josef righted an old chair and sat near him.

"Son, I know the rumor has bothered you as well as it has me, but if there is one thing I have learned in this life, it's that rumors and gossip are empty words. We have to be positive."

"Papa, I can't . . ."

Josef took a deep breath and interrupted, "I want to tell you something I've always remembered.

"I was sitting on my father's lap by the fireplace, watching the smoke from his pipe swirl in the air, creating weird shapes and images. I listened as he told me a story I've never forgotten, a story about a great elephant.

"'This elephant,' my father began, 'was the biggest ever seen. She must have weighed more than four tons, and stood twelve feet tall, yet she was gentle as a mouse. But, even though she had been known to pull, push, and carry more than any other elephant, the one thing that made her famous was that she could perform her entire circus act without a trainer.'"

Bram gasped. He'd never heard of such a thing. "But, Papa, how did she know what to do and in what order to do it?"

"Well, son, this was no ordinary elephant. It is said that only one out of every ten thousand elephants has this special gift. They have something happening in their heads. Something we humans wouldn't understand. They know the ways of man."

"What was her name, Papa?" Bram asked.

Bram's father gazed out across the barn, lost in the memory of the past. "Modoc, my son. Modoc — the world's greatest elephant." Then Josef turned to look at Bram again, his eyes filled with emotion.

Modoc, Bram thought. That was Mosey's real name —

the name she'd been given at birth. "*Your* Modoc . . . Mosey is one of those very special elephants, Bram. That's why I gave her the same name as the Mosey of old. You and she were born on the same hour of the same day. But there is something more. You are both connected — in a very spiritual way."

Bram nodded. He didn't exactly understand how he and Mosey always knew when the other was in need. They were very protective of each other. They could even communicate in a special way, but he rarely told anybody about that.

Bram sensed that his father must have known the old Mosey as well as he knew this one. Something must have happened to cause the pain he saw in his father's face, but he thought it best to leave it alone.

Josef placed the chamois cloth bundle in Bram's lap. Bram unfolded it slowly, knowing that whatever it contained was very dear to his father. Inside lay a wooden hand-carved silver-tipped bull hook. A series of carvings ran down its length depicting men and elephants in different poses. A line of initials was engraved on the inner side of the shaft. Bram noticed that the last one was freshly carved: *B.G.*

"Bram, this bull hook has been handed down for many

generations from one trainer to another. Trainers who had special elephants like Mosey used it wisely."

Bram ran his hand over the engraved images. He could hear the voices of the great mahouts and their elephants. He also realized what an honor it was to be given this prized possession — an honor and an affirmation that he, Bram, would one day become a trainer worthy of using it.

A year ago, when he was twelve and had become an apprentice trainer, his father showed him how to handle a bull hook. Bram thought it was a horrible name, but his father explained how many years ago trainers called it that. They used to call the elephants "bulls," and because the stick has a hook, it became the "bull hook."

"It is used as an extended hand," Josef had said. "The elephants are so big and strong that they don't feel human hands other than when you pet them. Hence, something stronger was needed." He continued. "Commands like, leg up, stop, go, come, down, stand, and so forth can be emphasized gently using a bull hook. Sometimes, bad trainers used it to hit the elephants, but the best were too respectful of their animals to do so."

Bram's eyes filled with tears as he looked from the bull hook to his father. "I only hope I can follow in the footsteps of these great men," he said softly.

"Remember, Bram, it is not a weapon — it is a tool to guide and to teach. This is a difficult time for you and Mosey. We don't know what tomorrow may bring, but whatever it does, whether good or bad, it will lead you to another point in your life where your special gift will be realized. Mosey will survive, and so will you. Go with the faith that whatever happens will be the correct way."

Josef wrapped his arms around Bram. "Go be all you can be, my boy." Josef held his son, his silent tears running down his cheeks.

Bram was crying too. "I love you so much, Papa. You are the best father a son could have."

It was two days since Bram had heard the rumor about the circus being sold. Three candles lit the corner of the Gunterstein barn. Bram finished blanketing Mosey for the night, then joined Curpo and String, who were sitting on some hay bales. String sat on two so his knees wouldn't be in the way. Their shadows depicted them as unearthly creatures.

Finally, his voice barely a whisper, Bram asked, "What are we going to do, Curpo?"

"I don't know." Curpo scooted down off the bale and began pacing, then stopped. "Maybe . . . maybe there's a way you could buy 'er. We could all pitch in and 'ave enough to —"

"Not in a million years," interrupted String. "Don't elephants cost a lot of money? And besides, whoever buys the circus will buy everything — the animals, tents, equipment, the whole lot."

"And what about the performers?" asked Bram.

"Staying here," String said. "That's what I heard."

"But . . . what about you and Curpo — how can they possibly replace you?"

"There're other people who will take our jobs," String said.

"That's awful." Bram sighed. "How can they do that?"

String looked down at the dejected boy and said, "We don't know for certain that the circus will be sold. Let's just wait and see."

"I 'ear there's a chance the circus will go overseas," piped Curpo.

Bram got down off the bale and went over to adjust Mosey's blanket. "Look, there is no way I'm losing Mosey," Bram stated emphatically. "No matter what."

Nobody spoke for a moment. Suddenly, String stood up, almost hitting his head on a low-hanging rafter. "I've got it!" he said excitedly. "Work for them."

"Who?" asked Bram.

"The new owners."

Bram looked up at String. "But you said they're not hiring performers."

"You don't have to be a performer."

Bram's face brightened. "You're right — I can do anything — a roustabout, a keeper, concession helper, whatever it takes — as long as I'm with Mosey."

"Well, then, there's only one thing left to do, mate," said Curpo, reaching to pat Bram on the back.

"What's that?" asked Bram.

"You have to get hired first."

 **FOUR**

Dear Herr Gunterstein,

Due to my poor health, the strain of operating the circus has become too much. My doctor has advised me to leave for a warmer climate. Therefore, I wish to inform you that I will be selling the circus.

Thank you for your years of faithfulness and dedication. Please see that all your personal belongings are removed from the circus location by the same day next month, as all animals, equipment, and vehicles are being offered for sale immediately.

Sincerely,
Franz Gobel

"So, it's true," Curpo said, handing the letter back to Bram.

Curpo was in the back of the truck, cleaning it out, when Bram came in and showed the letter to him.

Bram said nothing. He had no words. Ever since yesterday, when his father had received the letter, he couldn't face the fact that it was really going to happen. His father tried to console him, but there was little Josef could do. He was as devastated by the news as Bram. Katrina said nothing, worried for them both.

Curpo thought for a moment. "Ya know, Bram, yer've been my friend for a long time. When things are good we share. When they take a turn for the worse I feel the pain as yer do. This is a horrible thing that is 'appening. Now, I don't know where it will lead, but we are both fighters and I just know that something will turn this around." He put he hand on Bram's shoulder, "You'll see, my friend."

"I hope so, Curpo," said Bram. "I hope so."

The word was out that Mr. North, a wealthy circus owner, had purchased the circus and would be taking it over to the United States. Herr Gobel had asked Josef to show the act to Mr. North and his animal trainer. But ever since he had heard that the circus was being sold and other trainers were to work with the animals, Josef had taken a turn for the worse. He was now hemorrhaging from his coughing. The doctor said he had developed tuberculosis. Being as sick he was, Josef asked Bram to take his place. Bram knew the act, as he had helped his father teach the elephants their behaviors, and felt confident he could do a good job.

For two days Bram waited for the new owner to arrive. Afraid of missing him, he spent most of the time in the menagerie tent. Gertie visited one day, bringing him some of his favorite nut-and-raisin bread that she had made. Even Mosey had a few slices. Bram and Gertie sat in the hay, leaning against Mosey's leg. Mosey lowered her trunk, encircling them both. Her belly rumbles could barely be heard. There was no need for talking.

Early in the afternoon of the third day, Bram sat in the curl at the end of Mosey's trunk as she gently rocked him back and forth, much like a mother would her child. Bram wrapped a blanket around his shoulders. The weather had taken a turn for the worse. Dark clouds had moved in, covering the countryside with a light rain. The elephants were shivering. Bram and Curpo laid some blankets over their backs to keep them warm.

Then Bram changed into his best keeper outfit and walked up and down, awaiting the new owner's arrival.

Curpo's eyes followed him back and forth until he started to get dizzy.

"Bram, do yer mind? Sit down for a spell — I'm feelin' a bit woozy from watchin' you!"

"Oh, Curpo, what if they say no? What will I do?"

Curpo got up and went over to Bram. He grabbed his hand to stop him from pacing. "Look, Bram, one thing at a time. Whatever 'appens, we'll 'andle it."

A shiny black limousine squeaked to a halt outside the tent. Bram tightened his grip on Curpo's hand. Three men got out of the car. The driver held the flap of the tent while the other two entered, then returned to the car. There were no introductions.

"Where is the trainer?" demanded a tall, distinguished man sporting a thick mustache.

"Here I am, sir," Bram answered, a nervous twitch quite apparent in his speech. "Well, that is, my Papa is, but he's sick so I came to show the act."

"Fine, fine, do it," the man answered impatiently.

"Don't you want to hear about the elephants? Their names and — ?"

"Excuse me, Mr. North," said the other man. "We'll be changing their names so it won't matter."

"But you can't change their names! I mean, they already have them and . . . well, they only answer to . . . their . . . names, sir."

"What is *your* name, son?" interrupted Mr. North.

"Bram, sir. Bram Gunterstein."

"Hmmm! All right, *Mr. Gunterstein,* so do the act!" His face had turned very red.

Bram tripped on the hose in a hurried effort to please. Curpo undid the leg chains while Bram readied the pedestals that the elephants performed on. For the next twenty minutes Bram put the elephants through their routine. There were times when the thought crossed his mind to do a bad job. Then maybe they wouldn't buy Mosey. But his upbringing would never allow that.

When he had finished, the men started out the door without any comment. He heard the one say to Mr. North he'd change Mosey's name to Jumbo. Bram ran after them.

"Please, sir, may I go with them as their trainer?"

Mr. North stopped and turned. "Why would I have a boy like you as a trainer? I already have the best." He looked toward the other man who smiled, showing two missing teeth.

"But, sir." Bram caught Mr. North's arm. "I can't be without Mosey."

He looked at Bram's hand on his arm. Bram could feel the heat coming from his anger and quickly removed it. Mr. North looked directly into Bram's eyes.

"No! The answer is no! Hear me, boy. No! You're a nosey brat. You're of the wrong *tribe*, you hear me? Now get!"

The men got into the car and drove off. Bram realized that his chances of being with Mosey in the future were gone. His tears mingled with the light rain.

Bram stood there shivering. His mind whirled. "The wrong tribe?" he questioned. "What wrong tribe?"

A man emerged from the shadows. "You're Jewish, Bram. And he's prejudiced."

"I don't understand. What's prejudice?"

"Some people don't like certain people. Maybe because of their color or race, even how they talk. My name's Kelly, Kelly Hanson, what's yours?"

"Bram Gunterstein, Mosey's trainer. She's one of the elephants that performs here."

"Well, I'd better be on my way," said Kelly.

Bram said, "I was just thinking — wait until Mr. North finds out."

"Finds out what?"

"Mosey's Jewish."

 **FIVE**

That night Bram lay in bed thinking about Mosey. What would they do without each other? They had grown up together. He had made certain nobody ever harmed her. Would she be safe apart from him? He went to sleep praying that he would find an answer.

When Bram awoke he heard murmurs outside his bedroom door. He hurriedly got dressed and started downstairs, only to see Dr. Vollen speaking in a quiet tone to his mother at the front door. A soothing handshake and he was gone. Katrina leaned against the wall and sobbed quietly.

"Mother, what's wrong?" Bram approached slowly,

afraid to hear her answer. Katrina put her arms around her son.

"The doctor says your father may die."

Bram held his mother as she cried, feeling the heart-breaking emotion quake through her body. He couldn't even imagine what his life would be like without his father. All that he was or would ever be came from him. Josef had taught him everything he knew about life, nature, and the way to reach into an animal's heart and find that special love few humans can ever know.

As he got ready for bed that night, Bram thought about his life. Everything had been going so well until now. His life was full of caring people, a beautiful farm, the circus, and Mosey. And now, his father was deathly ill, the circus had been sold, and Mosey would be going to a far-off country.

Why, God? he silently questioned. He needed to find an inner strength to take on the challenges that faced him. Did such strength come to you automatically at a certain age? Or was it brought about by changes you made in your life?

Bram stayed awake a long time, mulling these things over. This was a time for making decisions himself, he finally realized. To be a man meant taking on responsibilities. That was the difference.

He went upstairs to his parents' bedroom, which was

cloaked in shadows. Josef lay in bed. Bram went to the bed and gently sat on its edge.

"Papa?"

Nothing.

"Papa, it's Bram."

A barely audible voice spoke. "I'm here, son."

Bram couldn't believe how quickly his father had aged. His face, which had once looked so strong and wise, had become gray, withered, and marked with deep lines. His breathing was labored and raspy. Josef opened his eyes. The bright lights that Bram had once seen in them were dim and fading.

"Bram, my boy, come close."

Bram felt his eyes begin to tear as he lay close to his father.

"Papa, you're not going to leave us, are you?"

Josef sighed deeply. "Life is a big circle. We never know where we are in the circle — at the beginning or end. Whatever happens will be right. It may not seem so at the time, but it's God's will." Josef continued, "Now then, how is Mosey?"

"She's fine, Papa, just fine."

A faint smile broke across his father's solemn, pale lips. "Ah! I taught you well. You don't know how to lie! Never did."

Bram's eyes misted over. "I can handle her, Papa. But they won't let me. I don't want her to leave."

Josef held his son. "Listen to me." His cough grew more insistent. "This is the time to listen to your heart. Do what you think is right."

A coughing seizure came over him then, and he gasped for air. Heart pounding, Bram held his father until the coughing subsided.

Josef's voice was now a whisper. "Bram, take care of Mosey. Take care of . . . Mo . . ."

Bram got up from the bed, tucking the blankets around his father. He looked around the room. The shadows were more prominent now. He went to the door, turning back once to look at his father's still, sleeping form. Then he slowly closed the door.

# SIX

On a gray cloudy day Josef was buried in a little cemetery on a hill not far from the farm. People came from miles around. Dozens of cars lined the narrow dirt road. The sideshow people had borrowed the calliope and towed it up behind the circus horses so Josef could have the music he loved at his funeral. Even Mosey was there. Josef's whole life had been elephants, and Mosey was one of his favorites. Herr Gobel had to beg Mr. North to allow Bram to take Mosey, and he finally agreed.

Bram, Curpo, and Gertie rode Mosey, dressed in black as a sign of respect. They took a shortcut through the forest where they picked field flowers, and fashioned a wreath that Bram hung on Mosey's neck. They arrived at the top of a nearby hill overlooking the cemetery as the calliope's music echoed across the valley.

They sat on Mosey, looking down at the many people trudging up the hill. There was Bolt, the Electric Man; Josephine, the Bearded Lady; Marigold, the Torso Lady; Mesmera, the Snake Lady; and of course, String, with his long legs taking giant strides. Lilith, the Fat Lady, came in a cart pulled by the circus ponies.

Bram eased Mosey down the hill toward the cemetery and brought her up to where Katrina, close friends, and relatives were standing. Mosey bowed low to assist Bram as he slid off. Then Bram helped Gertie and Curpo down, and they all stood with Bram's mother as the rabbi spoke. Bram heard the words but got lost in the meaning. He was imagining his father inside the coffin. A hard knot had formed in his stomach but the tears wouldn't come. He didn't know why.

Katrina placed a bouquet of red and white roses on the coffin. After a nudge from Bram, Mosey reached up with her trunk, took the wreath off her neck, stepped forward, and laid it at the foot of the coffin.

The calliope played Josef's favorite circus song. As evening came on, the sky darkened. The three friends rode Mosey back up to the top of the hill. Looking down they saw the long line of the mourners heading home.

Mosey raised her trunk. A low belly rumble ended in a forlorn trumpet that was heard across the hills into the valley to the very circus grounds that Josef had loved. It was her final good-bye.

## SEVEN

Things were never the same after Josef died. It seemed as if he had taken the life out of all that was dear to Katrina. Strong woman that she was, she fought to keep things in order and the farm running. She was helped by a fair sum of insurance money that Josef had arranged for her.

One morning, a week after the funeral, Bram's friends gathered in the barn to help with the chores. Bram had arranged bales of hay in a semicircle so everyone could have a place to sit.

"Thanks for coming," he told them. "It's really nice of you all to help out. Since Papa's death, it's been hard doing all that's needed to be done on the farm. I guess things will let up a bit when the circus and . . . well" —

he hesitated — "everything is gone." There was a moment of silence.

"So, let's get busy," said Bram, cutting through the heavy silence that followed the thought. As though someone had rung a bell, everybody moved at the same time only in different directions. Hay was stacked, grain mixed, leather elephant gear was soaked in oils. The barn was swept from one end to the other.

Curpo rode on String's shoulders to change burned-out lightbulbs high in the rafters.

"Wow, it's sure 'igh up here. I'm glad I'm short," said Curpo as he swayed precariously on String's shoulders. "There's not much oxygen at this height. Now I see why yer so dizzy all the time."

"It's better then worrying if a cat will think you're a —!" String swayed.

"Ah! Don't even say it," said Curpo, giving a friendly sharp tug on his hair.

A burst of sparks flashed from the breaker switches and lit up the back of the barn for a moment.

"Bolt, what are you doing? Are you okay?" yelled Bram.

"Yah, sure. Just go about your own business," he snapped back. Everybody broke up giggling.

"I'm surprised he doesn't electrocute himself," laughed Josephine.

Then there was a lull. Suddenly Marigold began to sing, her lilting soprano voice resonating throughout the old wooden barn, echoing from every corner and crevice. The early morning rays of light shone through some of the broken boards and rafters, bursting forth into a myriad of bright colors. For just a moment, her singing had transformed the old barn into a cathedral.

After the funeral, the new owner forbade Bram from taking Mosey off the circus property. So every day he made the trip to the circus grounds to be with her and Emma and the others. He missed not being able to go on the rides they used to take to the forest or the river, where Curpo and Gertie would help him stretch Mosey out and then they'd all sit on her belly and pick ticks from her skin.

A month went by, and the weather was turning cool. One Friday morning, Bram had gotten to the circus grounds a bit early when a gruff voice rang out, "Hey, you! Where ya going?"

"I'm headed to the jumbos' tent to see my elephant, Mosey."

"No elephant called Mosey here. Aren't you the kid that the boss told to stay out?"

"But, you don't understand."

"No, *you* don't understand! Out! Now!"

The man grabbed Bram's arm and started to pull him to the exit gate. Bram pulled away.

"Look, I'm her trainer. I can help."

"You're talking to the wrong person, son. The new trainer started working here just this morning. And for your information, this elephant you call Mo . . ."

"Mosey."

"Yeah, well, whatever, her name is now Jumbo."

With this the man grabbed Bram's arm again and this time Bram offered no resistance. He was devastated.

That night Bram sat in his room, thinking of all that had occurred in the past month. The knot that had been in his stomach ever since his father died unraveled. All the pain and hurt surfaced and the tears that he had held back gushed forth.

He cried for the unfairness of it all. His father had been a good man and shouldn't have been taken away so soon. The selling of Mosey was wrong. She had been happy at the farm and in the forest, and loved the people around her. Now she was to be taken away by strangers to a foreign land. Bram fell asleep curled up on the floor until the early morning sunlight filled his room. He awoke feeling different. Better.

He knew the time for an important decision was at

hand. During the last couple of weeks, he'd been pondering whether or not to stow away on the ship that would take the circus to America, to risk being found out and maybe even thrown overboard or set ashore in some strange country. Even worse, to be put in jail, never to see Mosey again.

He had to try. It was worth the risk. She was the most important thing in his life. And then, he had an obligation to his father, whose final words had been, "Take care of Mo."

So, he made his decision. Yes, he would start making his plans today! Then he thought of his mother. She would be anguished. But, if he could get to America and get settled, someday he'd bring her over.

Saying good-bye to her and to his friends would be the hardest thing of all. He erased the thought. I'll deal with that tomorrow.

Bram got up early. He dressed, grabbed a quick breakfast, gave his mother a peck on the cheek, and was out the door. He had a lot to do. First he had to find out when the ship was leaving and where it was leaving from. He took his bicycle and headed for the circus. Upon arriving, he found String and asked him to meet him at the elephant tent as soon as he could. He rode around the back of the circus grounds and stopped outside the fence behind the elephant tent.

Hiding his bike in some nearby bushes, he crawled through a hole that Curpo had cut for him so he could visit Mosey. He ran across the clearing and dove under the tent flap, nearly scaring her to death!

"Mosey, it's me!" Bram stood up, dusting the hay from his clothes. Her belly rumbled as she gave a loud trumpet and stretched her leg chain as far as she could. She encircled her trunk around his waist and pulled him toward her.

"I brought you a goody," said Bram, pulling out a big red apple. Mosey wrapped the tip of her trunk around it and put it in her mouth.

"Hey, Bram, what yer up to, mate?" asked Curpo, who was raking up the hay.

Bram was pleased that the circus people had allowed Curpo to stay and take care of the elephants until they left.

"Hi! Curpo, how's Mosey doing?"

"She was off her feed for a while, but since I've been 'ere she's gone back on and is doing well."

"Curpo, do you know when the ship is sailing?"

"Sunday, two weeks from tomorrow. That's when we'll all be out of a job. The caravan will pull out of the circus grounds heading for the port at about midnight. They think it will take about four full days of driving to get there."

The flap of the tent opened. String entered, bending low to come through. The three sat down on the elephant pedestals.

Bram revealed his plan to stow away on the ship. The conviction in his voice surprised even him. He spoke of all the things that brought him to making this decision.

"Father told me, on his deathbed, to take care of Mosey."

"What about your mum?" Curpo asked.

"And the farm?" added String.

"I wouldn't be doing this, but with the insurance that Papa left, Mama will have enough money to hire help — and you two need jobs now, so it'll work. And I'll feel so much better knowing you're there to take care of her."

"Aren't you afraid of being caught?" String asked.

"I don't want to think about that — I just know I have to be with Mosey. And she needs to be with me!"

"Okay, but what about when you reach America? Mr. North has already said no, that you can't work for them."

"Somehow, I'll change his mind."

Curpo smiled. "I bet you will."

Curpo and String were his best friends; they understood what he was going through and agreed. Although his plan was dangerous, he knew it was the thing to do.

The following evening, the group plotted the best way for Bram to stow away.

"Now, 'ere's the plan," said Curpo, who had perched himself on a couple of hay bales so he could talk with the others eye to eye.

"String and I will find out which is the best truck to hide in so that you don't attract the attention of the workers while they are loading the equipment."

"Do you think I could ride with Mosey?" asked Bram.

"I doubt it. The elephant trucks are all locked up. There's no way in," said Curpo.

"I met one of the guys who works for the circus. He's offered to help," said String.

"What?" Bram shouted. "You told someone I'm going to stow away? How could you? They might try to stop me . . . or tell someone!"

"Bram, lower your voice, someone might hear you." He leaned over and touched Bram's head reassuringly. "It's all right, I trust him. Besides, he told me that the ship is so huge, it would be very difficult to get on without help."

"Well, what's done is done. When do I meet him?"

"At the dock. He said it's too dangerous to meet sooner."

"How will I know him?"

"He'll know you," Sting said cryptically.

As the friends parted they agreed that on the night when the circus was to leave, String and Curpo would meet Bram on the road in front of his house and go with him to the circus grounds.

They only had two weeks to gather information about where the ship was sailing, what route the caravan was taking, and how many trucks were going. They had to find out the order in which the trucks would line up. String offered to use his car to take them to the embarking area at the circus grounds.

Finally, it was the day of the caravan's departure. Bram snuck into the tent to visit Mosey one last time. "Mosey, tonight is it." She swayed gently from side to side as Bram spoke. "Just in case something happens — I mean, nothing will — but just in case, you go on with the circus. Now, it might be tough. These people do things differently. But don't fight back."

Mosey listened to every word, swinging slowly until Bram said, "I'm going to try to come with you, but if I don't make it, you just go on without me." Bram put his arms around her, smothering his tears in her trunk. "I love you, Mosey, you hear, and I'll be with you always, in my heart."

Bram felt the tension in her trunk as she raised him slowly up to her eye. Whatever love can be shown between an animal and a person was expressed at that moment.

Bram put his cheek against Mosey's. He looked into her eye. It appeared as a deep pool of liquid light. He felt he was sinking into it, down into her world. Bram felt Mosey was trying to tell him something. Something important that would always be with him. The words came to him.

*We are as one, never to be separated.*

The words were engraved in Bram's mind. Mosey lowered Bram slowly. Only when his feet touched the floor did he awaken to his full senses. It was as though he had been in a dream. Bram knew at that moment that no matter how far apart they were, they would always be together in heart and spirit.

# EIGHT

In his room that evening, Bram set out the things he felt would be needed for the journey: the bull hook his father had given him, a pocket knife, a few shirts, two pairs of pants, some shorts, underpants, undershirts, socks, a jacket, cap, shoes, handkerchief, comb, pen, and a pad of paper. From his glass fruit jar he pulled all the money he had saved from helping his father.

Bram hadn't yet told his mother he was leaving. He could no longer put it off, but what should he say? No mother would let her thirteen-year-old go on such a journey.

Bram loved his mother very much. She was loving and gentle and had brought him up to be the same. Yet she was also very strong. Katrina had always been the backbone of the family, and running the farm, managing the money, and caring for Bram and his father when they were ill had, in Bram's eyes, made her a saint. He knew that she could survive while he was gone. And, deep down, he felt she would understand — or was that just his hopeful imagination?

He decided to write a letter. He wanted to talk with her but he just couldn't bring himself to tell her that he was stowing aboard a freighter heading for America. She might prevent him from going and he couldn't risk that happening.

It was the stroke of nine, still three hours before the circus trucks were to depart. For the tenth time he read his note:

*My dear Mother,*

*Please do not worry about me. I have gone to be with Mosey. Papa's right — we have to be together, and I want to honor Papa's wish to take care of her. I know you will be fine; you have Curpo to take care of you, and the others from the circus are always ready to help. I will get a job assisting the new elephant trainer and be with Mosey. When I get settled, I'll contact you. I'll save enough money for you and Gertie to join me, and maybe even Curpo too. Thank you, Mama, for being the best mother a son could have. I'll miss you.*

*Love, your son,*
*Bram*

He folded the note and placed it inside his desk.

Bram and his mother had a quiet dinner, talking of how things were when Josef was alive. After dinner, Bram finished a couple of helpings of his favorite apple strudel. She gave him a warm hug and whispered, "You do what you have to do."

She kissed him on the cheek and turned quickly to wash the dishes. Bram sensed that she was holding back tears. She knew! She knew! No one had told her but mothers were like that. They knew things intuitively.

Evening had given way to night. It was cool and crisp as Bram, shouldering his pack, quietly closed the door behind him and headed down the dirt road to the car parked in the shadows. There String and Curpo waited. He had left the letter on his bed so his mother could find it. As they drove off, Bram thought he saw the curtains move in his bedroom. His mother's words, her voice, were fresh in his mind: *"You do what you have to do."*

They drove in silence for a little while.

"You still want to see Gertie?" asked String.

"Yeah, I do. I'll only be a few minutes."

String had had his car rebuilt to fit his unusual frame. His eight-foot-plus size could fit in the car only if he sat in the backseat. He'd taken out the driver's front seat and extended the steering wheel so he could drive from the back. Someone who didn't know String and his car would see no one in the driver's seat and would think the car was driving itself.

String let Bram out at the end of the lane that led to Gertie's house. He didn't want to wake her parents.

"I won't be long."

How do I tell her? Bram thought to himself as he headed toward the house. He had always loved her. At least what he thought was love. The people at the circus had teased him about it, but down deep he knew that when they grew up they would marry and have children. They and Mosey would all live together.

The frost cracked under his feet as he made his way around the back of the house to the bedroom. He tapped on the window. A small light silhouetted Gertie as she came to the window, which was steamed up from the heat inside the room. Her hand wiped the steam away. When she saw it was Bram, a smile crossed her face as she attempted to open the window. With Bram helping from the outside, the frost that had been holding it shut broke away and the window slid open. Bram climbed over the sill and closed the window behind him.

"Bram, what are you doing here? Is something wrong?"

Gertie was shivering in her nightgown, either from the cold or concern for what Bram might tell her. Bram unbuttoned his coat and pulled her to him, wrapping his coat around her. She felt warm and secure nestled up in his warmth. He cupped her head, resting it against his chest.

"Gertie, I'm leaving. They're taking Mosey and I can't let her go without me."

"What!" Gertie tried to raise her head, but Bram held her tight.

"Please, let me finish. When Papa died, he made me promise to take care of Mosey. You know how much I love her. We'll die without each other. So I've decided I'm going to stow away on the ship that's taking her to America."

She raised her head. Tears were sliding down her cheeks. "Bram, I . . . I don't know what to say. I had always thought that someday we would —"

Bram cut her off. "Be married."

"Yes. Yes. Don't you love me, Bram?"

"I do. You know I do, and someday I will come back for you. Will you wait for me?" Bram asked, his eyes filled with tears.

"I'll wait and think of you every day until we are together."

Their faces, inches apart, melted together. Their kiss reached into their very souls, each knowing that the love they had for one another was strong enough to last.

"I love you so very much, Gertie." His hands brushed the hair from her face.

"You are my love. I know that our lives are linked together. My father told me once that in the book of destiny, all things that are to be are written. Our day will come when we will be together always." Again he kissed her tenderly. Tears flooded her eyes as she watched him head back to the car. It had started to snow. The flakes turned his blue coat into white as he disappeared into the night.

The car arrived at the circus grounds just as the first truck leading the caravan was pulling out. String turned into a dark secluded area near where the trucks would be passing.

"Well, I guess this is it," said Bram, his voice a bit shaky.

"Yeah, now that the time for yer leaving has come," said Curpo, "how do yer feel?"

"Terrible. My stomach is turning in knots. Gosh, I hope this is the right thing to do." Then he had an afterthought, "Who loaded Mosey?"

"That new fellow, the guy without the front teeth."

"Which truck is she in?"

"The one with the red trim," said String, pointing to the last truck in the convoy. "She has plenty of room, so she'll be okay."

The trucks had started their engines and were slowly pulling out.

Bram gathered his stuff. "Which is the truck I'm gonna get in?"

"That one there," String said, pointing to a truck with an American flag on the antenna and a canvas flap covering the back. "My friend left it undone so you could climb in."

"When you make a run for the truck," said String, "we'll flash our lights in another direction to keep the workers' attention away from you." He handed Bram a sack. "Here, take this, it's food for your trip."

"Thanks, String," said Bram. "Tell everyone good-bye. I'll miss them. Thanks for helping." He shook String's hand. "You've been a good friend — a bit tall, but a good friend."

All three chuckled, but the next moment they were clearing their throats and swallowing to keep the tears at bay.

Curpo spoke up, "You take care out there. Be sure and write."

"I will."

Bram opened the door and stepped out. Curpo stood up on the seat so he could look out the window.

"Oh! I 'most forgot." He handed Bram a small pouch. "Just a few things to remember me by. Bubblegum, toothpicks, yer know, all those important things."

The same hard knot that Bram felt in his stomach when his father died had returned.

"Good-bye Curpo, my dear friend. Take care of Mother and the farm, okay?"

"We'll take care of yer mother and the farm, yer take care of our girl, now, ya 'ear?" answered Curpo. "And don't worry, yer doing the right thing, Bram. You are my brother and I'll never forget you," said Curpo.

He lifted the gold chain and medallion from his neck and put it over Bram's head. Bram burst out crying. Reaching through the open car window, he hugged Curpo tight.

"Curpo, I . . ." Their tears mingled as their cheeks touched.

"I lov ya, guy, now get on with it," said Curpo, his voice barely audible. Bram wiped his face and grabbing his pack, stood there. "Now go, ya hear. Go!"

The truck that Bram was to hop into was coming up. As it approached, he threw his pack in, then jumped in after it. He quickly closed the flap and sat down in the dark on the floor with his back to some bales of hay. Through a rip in the canvas he could see the car. Its head-lights flashed a good-bye as his friends disappeared from view.

A noise close by startled him. A match was struck, lighting up the face of an unshaven vagabond sitting alongside of him. He lit his cigarette then smiled a tooth-less grin as the match burned out.

## NINE

The four-day trip was a tiring, bumpy ride that stopped only for meals and toilet breaks.

The drivers slept in their rigs, some in the back, others in the cab. String's friend must have known that the driver of the truck Bram was in always slept in the cab. Occasionally, he would check the back, but seeing as it only carried circus paraphernalia, there wasn't much need.

Bram tried to speak to the vagabond a few times, but the man would only smile his toothless grin. Bram figured he was not very smart. Maybe he couldn't even talk. The man would wait until the truck had come to a stop at a restaurant before he would slip off to relieve himself in the nearby bushes. Bram did the same except for those occasions when he could go into a café and use their rest room. Some of the drivers mistook him for another worker and offered him a bit of their food.

On the second night of the journey, Bram dared to sneak over to the elephant truck and watch until the driver and trainer had gone to eat. Then he jumped in and talked with Mosey, reassuring her that all was going to be okay. He sat in the semidark, talking, touching her trunk, reassuring her that all was well. His mind explored the special rapport they had with each other. Each could feel the other's thoughts.

Later, as he lay sleepless in the back of his moving, rattling truck, Bram remembered the time he took sick and Mosey knew, even though Bram was in his room and she was in the barn. His father had told him the story many times.

"Well, I woke with a start. I heard something. Again the sound, a loud trumpet. It was Mosey, and I knew something was wrong! I woke up Katrina. 'There's something wrong with Mosey,' I said as I raced downstairs three steps at a time.

"When I jerked open the door there was Mosey in a state of panic. She had broken down the barn door and busted the link that held her leg chain in the ground. She was dragging her chain, racing up and down in front of the house trumpeting, ears forward, tail up. Then she started to push on the side of the house!

"I heard your mother yelling, 'Where's Bram? Josef, where is Bram?'

"I ran upstairs and threw open the door. I saw you lying kitty-corner on the bed. All the covers were on the floor. I picked you up. You were unconscious and sweating profusely. I yelled to your mother, 'The boy's sick! Get the keys to the car. We've got to get him to the hospital!'

"I wrapped you in a blanket and carefully carried you downstairs and out the door and ran to the car. Mosey ran alongside me, trumpeting, trying to put the tip of her trunk under the blanket to touch you to see if you were all right. Your mother had started the car and was sitting on the passenger side so that she could hold you on her lap while I drove. I handed you to her, jumped into the driver's side, and sped off with Mosey running alongside, trying to stick her trunk into the open window.

"I remember Curpo calling to her, 'Mosey, come on back, girl, come on now. There's nothing we can do.'

"In my rearview mirror I saw them walking back to the barn.

"For two weeks you lay in the hospital bed on the edge of death. The doctor said you had contracted a serious virus. Only a few people in the area had come down with it. Some had died. You were in a coma, unaware of what was going on around you. You had to be fed through a tube in your arm. Your mother and I took turns watching and caring for you every day and night. Gertie and Curpo came to help.

"During one visit, Curpo and your mother started to talk about Mosey. It was simple talk. How Mosey had gone off her feed and didn't have much energy ever since you left. Curpo said something about her mourning you.

"Whether it was the name Mosey or what they were saying about her being sick that penetrated your subconscious state no one knew, but when they looked around, you were sitting up looking at them! Katrina and Curpo rushed to your side. You smiled. Your first words were, 'How's Mosey?'

"Then, about a week later, at the farm, while Curpo was feeding Mosey, she stopped and let out a loud blast. She knew you were coming home! And sure enough you were. Down the driveway you ran, into the barn. I remember you screamed, 'Mosey!'

"She trumpeted as you sprang up onto her trunk, hugging and holding her. Mosey swung you in a big circle around and around, chirping and belly rumbling all the time. What a wonderful sight that was. You sat with her for many hours, sharing all that had happened to you while you were in the hospital, and Mosey stood quietly, listening to every word.

"You believed that she understood. And that night, watching you both, we all did. Maybe because the relationship you both share is different from any that had ever been seen or heard before. You might have died if she hadn't awakened me that fateful night. No one ever understood how Mosey could have known that you were in trouble."

The truck slammed to an abrupt stop. Jolted back to the present, Bram felt himself starting to shake. Had someone told about him being there? What if he was found? They might just put him out on the road to get home on his own. And what about Mosey? She would be on her own and . . . He felt a chill. Not from the cold air blowing in but from the horrible thoughts he was having. The more he dwelled on them, the more real they seemed. He parted the canvas and watched a cow slowly crossing the road. He figured the truck had swerved to avoid hitting the cow. Bram sat back and let out a big sigh.

He opened the small pouch that Curpo had given him. Inside he found various items that had been gathered through the years. A letter that Bram had written to Curpo while recovering in the hospital. The penknife that Bram had thought he had lost. Bram chuckled when he saw bubble gum. Curpo had also included a small diary and pen, and Bram's favorite chocolate.

He touched the medallion around his neck and pressed it to his cheek. It seemed to bring Curpo closer to him.

The memories only made him miss his mother and friends all the more. There were many times when he used to yearn to travel the world to see and meet people and visit their countries. But this wasn't what he had imagined. Even though this was his first day in the truck, he felt as if he had been gone a long time. He sat for hours, watching the scenery go by. The warm weather during the day turned very cold at night. He broke open a hay bale and made a bed. Although it helped to keep him warm, he itched and scratched all night. He knew it couldn't be the hay that caused him to itch. He had slept in hay many nights at the farm with Mosey without a problem. It must be the vagabond. He was always scratching his head, and whenever he passed Bram to go outside during a gasoline stop, he smelled of old laundry. Maybe the old man had lice or something. Just the thought of it made Bram itch even more.

The line of trucks, like a giant snake, wound its way along the country roads, crossing great distances. The accents he heard at the truck stops told him they had passed into another country. Even the houses and cars looked strange and different. The mountains disappeared from view as the trucks headed southeast. The motion of the truck was hypnotic. Bram would doze off, thinking of his life back home and how it had changed. His thoughts drifted to Gertie. She used to crawl through the old drainage pipe that led from the front of the roadway to the house, then hide around the corner of the house and watch when he brought Mosey out of the barn.

He remembered the first day they met, two years earlier. He was lying on his back on top of Mosey, getting a bit of sun. He often did this, his feet hooked under Mosey's ears after he had finished his chores. He had his shirt off, soaking up the warmth, when he heard a voice:

"Hi, up there!"

It came as such a surprise he almost rolled off Mosey.

"Who's that?" he asked looking right, left, back, front, and seeing no one.

"It's me."

"Who's me?"

"Me, Gertie, I'm down here."

Bram looked over Mo's head and there, down below, was this thin imp of a girl hanging on to Mosey's trunk. Gertie's blond hair hung to the middle of her back. Her large brown eyes reminded Bram of the young fawn's he had seen in the forest. And when she smiled, the curl at the corner of her mouth told him she was full of secrets and mischief. Bram couldn't take his eyes off her.

"What are you doing?" he asked.

"I'm playing."

"You're not afraid?"

"No, I've been watching for a long time, weeks, and I see how affectionate Mosey is."

"You know her name?"

"Sure, can I come up?"

"I guess so." Bram was completely surprised by her bravery.

"How?" she asked.

Bram thought for a moment. "I'll have Mosey lower her head. You just grab her ears, put your foot on her trunk, and she'll bring you up. Okay?"

"Okay." Gertie took a deep breath.

"Head down, Mo!" said Bram. Mosey lowered her head. Gertie grabbed Mosey's ears, put her foot on her trunk and in one swing, Mosey had her up as high as Bram. He grabbed her hand and helped her cross over onto Mosey's broad back, careful that she didn't step on her eye. Bram scooted back a bit to give her some room.

"Wow! It's sure high up here," Gertie said.

"You want to go for a ride?" asked Bram.

"Yeeess!" answered Gertie, full of enthusiasm.

"Move up, Mo!" said Bram, giving a gentle nudge with his feet. Mosey started forward with a lurch, causing Gertie to lose her balance and fall back against Bram. He quickly wrapped his arms around her so she wouldn't fall. She didn't seem to mind. In fact, he noticed a slight smile at the corner of her mouth. Maybe she wasn't so afraid of falling after all.

# TEN

On the morning of the fourth day Bram woke up to a new odor. It was in the air, and his nostrils were filled with a freshness he had never known. As the truck came to a halt, he carefully stuck his head out through the canvas flaps. Strange birds flew overhead making squawking noises.

As far as he could see, the road was filled with trucks of all sizes. They were all wedged together, trying to go down a narrow road that headed toward what appeared to be the port.

Horns were honking, motors revving up, brakes squeaking. Policemen were blowing their whistles, trying to direct the traffic. Bram wondered how there could be any order to the chaos.

Then from the side air vent he saw it! The ocean! A blue vastness of water that stretched to the horizon. He felt like yelling in his excitement, but he didn't want anyone to notice him. Never in all his imagination did he believe it would be this big. "I wish Gertie was here to see this."

Ships were coming and going. Large white birds dived into the water and others perched on the wharf, as though waiting to be fed.

As his truck drove onto the pier, a man in a bright orange jacket waved the truck into position. As it backed into its prescribed slot, Bram could see the rest of the trucks lining up and beginning to unload their cargo.

When he felt the coast was clear, he threw his gear out the back of the truck then jumped down after it. He waved to the vagabond, who just kept smiling, and ran to hide behind some big crates.

At the end of the pier was a huge ship. Bram couldn't believe its size — it seemed as long as the circus grounds and as high as one of the pine trees out by Cryer Lake. Overhead, giant cranes loaded circus crates and equipment onto it. Bram saw a man coming toward the crate. Dropping down, he hid between two crates.

"Hey, you!" the man whispered. "You Bram?"

Bram was frozen with fear. To have come all this way

and suddenly to be found. Then, the man peeked between the crates.

"I'm String's friend," he said.

Bram took in a deep breath and smiled. "Yes, sir, I'm Bram."

The man pointed to a group of crates sitting on the wharf. "Now, listen carefully. In about ten minutes, a man will come by driving a tractor. He'll drop off a large crate that's open on top. When he signals you, jump in as quickly as you can. Got it?"

"Yes sir, but what if . . . ?" The man had disappeared into the crowd of dockworkers.

Bram waited till the right moment, then when he felt the coast was clear, he made a dash for the boxes.

A few minutes later, a tractor carrying a huge crate was headed directly toward him. He was thrilled to see that the driver of the tractor was Kelly Hanson. Strapping his pack onto his back, he got ready.

The tractor stopped and unloaded the crate within a few yards of him. Kelly gave Bram a nod. Bram was up and gone as the crate hit the pavement. It was much higher than he thought and he had to struggle to get to the top.

At last he jumped inside. There was equipment everywhere. Canvas tents, a piece of a ticket booth, chains, boxes of tools, and a large coil of thick rope. Bram pulled some of the thick tent canvas over his head, squished himself down, and lay quietly.

A few trucks carrying more equipment dumped circus paraphernalia on top of him. Among the items were a dozen or so steel tent stakes. They tumbled down, striking him all over his body. It hurt, but the heavy tent canvas prevented any injury. The sunlight disappeared as a large wooden cover was slid on top of the crate and nailed shut. Pitch darkness!

Bram felt a tug as the crate tilted, then scraped as it was dragged along the ground. He braced himself against the corner. Soon after, he had a feeling of floating. Bram pulled the canvas off, fought his way clear of all the debris that had fallen on him. At the other end of the crate a thin crack of light shone through. Bram put his eye to it and was amazed to find that he had been hoisted way up into the sky. He could see the whole city.

His mouth dropped opened. "What a fantastic place!" he whispered, still afraid to speak out loud.

The crate started to turn slowly in a circle, allowing him to see first the city then the vast blue ocean. Never had he imagined anything like this.

He felt like a king surveying his kingdom. As the crate turned — the city, the ocean, the city, the ocean — he felt himself getting dizzy. He sat down rather quickly. He broke into a sweat. Once, a couple of years ago, the acrobats had taken him up on the trapeze. They held him while the trapeze spun around and around. He was scared. He started to sweat and threw up. What if the rope broke?

Now he was sweating and having the same thoughts, only just as he felt he was about to vomit, the crate stopped spinning. He looked out through the crack. The crate was swaying just enough for him to see a large hole in the deck directly under the crate.

As the crane lowered him into the bowels of the ship, he wondered about Mosey. Had she been carried the same way? He worried that she would get scared and the men would beat her to obey. And yet, on second thought, he knew that whatever method they used would be safe because they wanted her for the circus. A hurt elephant wouldn't do them any good.

A heavy thump. The crate had been lowered into the bottom of the ship. He heard what he believed to be the upper door on the deck slide shut. Total darkness. He wondered if Kelly would be able to find him. What if he couldn't?

Usually, he wasn't afraid of the dark. He hadn't been since he was a very little boy. But this was different. Very different. It was so quiet. He could hear himself breathing, his heart beating. Bram shook all over. He thought about his loved ones: his mother, Gertie, Curpo, and String. Would they be all right? Would he ever see them again? He tried to think of other things to occupy his mind.

This ship is huge! he thought to himself. I can't wait to find out what it feels like when it is out to sea.

He remembered the toy boats he used to play with. He and Gertie would ride Mosey to Cryer Lake, a beautiful place near the flower fields. At one end of the lake there was a small stream that tumbled down the mountainside. Bram would put Mosey downstream while he and Gertie would stay upstream to float one of their miniature boats. Mosey caught the boat before it went over a steep waterfall and was lost in the turbulence. Then, they would do it all over again.

A loud horn blasted through the ship, startling him. Two, three times, then suddenly Bram felt a little woozy. The ship was moving! They were under way!

Later, Bram was jolted from his sleep by a loud noise, then footsteps. He listened. He couldn't see anything. Then a booming voice echoed through the hold.

"Hey, kid. Where are ya?"

It was Kelly!

"Over here! I'm over here," yelled Bram.

"Okay, I'll get you out."

Bram heard a clanging of what sounded like tools being dropped to the floor. Then a series of banging noises that made Bram hold his ears. Finally he could see a pair of strong hands pry loose the top board. A flashlight shone down into the darkness, and a face appeared at the rim of the crate.

"Hey there," Kelly said. "How about a hand up?"

Bram was never so glad to see anyone. He reached his hand up as high as he could, and Kelly grabbed it.

"Here we go!" said Kelly as he lifted Bram up the side and onto the top. Bram balanced himself there while Kelly jumped to the floor.

"Okay, son. Jump!"

Bram jumped. Kelly broke his fall before he hit the ground. This man was strong, Bram thought.

"How ya doing, lad?" he asked.

"Well, sir, it was pretty dark in there. I want to thank you, sir. So much." Then an afterthought. "How long was I in there?" he asked.

"Just overnight."

"It sure was dark. I hope I don't get you in any trouble. I know I shouldn't be here," said Bram, "but I need to be —"

"I know, son, I know why you're here. Look, I don't want to kid you. What you have done is very brave and your loyalty to your elephant friend is admirable, but it's also dangerous. If they find you, you're finished. Captain Patel is a really tough character. Wants everything to be done by the book. To the letter of the law. So, whatever you do, don't get caught. I'll try to bring food to you each day. Stay low. Don't come up top on the deck for anything, you understand?"

"But what about Mosey? Is she okay?"

"She's fine, just fine. You have to stay here in the hold for now."

Kelly handed Bram a sack. "Here's a bit of food. It'll last till I can get down here again. I'll try to figure out how to get you to where they're keeping the elephants." Kelly placed a firm hand on Bram's shoulder. "You're a good kid," he said. Then he disappeared into the dark.

"See you later, Kelly."

Bram saw the wave of the flashlight in the dark and then it was gone.

## ELEVEN

For what seemed a very long time Bram stayed where Kelly had left him. He was glad to finally be out of the crate. Every once in a while the upper sliding door would open, letting in bright sunlight from above. Bram shielded his eyes, trying to see what was up there. Occasionally, a man hanging on to a huge crane hook that had a net wrapped around it was lowered into the hold.

A few times Bram heard a bit of muttering that had the word *elephant* in it. Boxes of supplies were loaded in the net and hauled back up to the deck. The door was then shut and the darkness closed in once more. Kelly was a good friend and brought him food almost every day.

Most of the time Bram couldn't tell if it was day or night. He slept a lot. His dreams were always of home.

"Look out, you'll fall!" Bram and Gertie were riding Mosey into the forest. Gertie had stood up on Mosey, planting her feet firmly on the largest part of the elephant's back, and began to dance.

"Look, Bram, I'm a circus dancer." She swayed to Mosey's movements. She wore a thin white dress with lace trim that hugged her small body at every turn. Her long, soft blond hair hung wild, sliding across her face, and her deep brown eyes peered from beneath, shining, sparkling, like the sun does when it moves in and out of the clouds. Bram watched for her smile at each pirouette. She turned and turned, closing her eyes, lost in the moment, and Bram knew she knew he was watching her every move. A slight dizziness caused her to falter and Bram quickly gathered her in, close and warm, as he settled down against Mosey's huge head. Bram held her tight even when it was no longer necessary. He put his cheek to hers. A slight turn and their lips met, gently. Mosey blew some dust from her eyes as they meandered toward the forest.

"Hey, Bram, wake up! Dinner."

Bram awoke to a bright light shining in his face. "Kelly?"

"Yeah, time to move on. But first, eat a bit to give you some strength. Sorry I couldn't make it down earlier. I was worried about ya."

"I'm all right, I guess. How long have I been down here?"

"It's been seven days since we left port."

"Any news about Mosey?"

"Sure is, son." Kelly smiled. "I'm going to take you to her right now!"

"What?"

"Yup. If we're lucky and quiet, we should be able to sneak by the crew and down into the next hold. That's where she's being kept."

Bram gulped down his food, nearly choking on a peanut butter sandwich. A quick drink of milk from a bottle and he was ready.

"Can't keep Mosey waiting," he said.

Kelly guided Bram through a dark corridor, up a long, steep staircase until they came out on the deck. The cold air took his breath away. The wind was blowing cold sprays of water across the ship. Huge waves were pounding her sides, but they didn't even bother her. He stood and took in several deep breaths of the crisp, fresh air and shivered at the thrill of being on deck.

"Bram, hurry up! Somebody's coming!" Kelly opened a door and they headed down another flight of stairs until they reached a curved tunnel. A strong natural odor filled Bram's nostrils, one he was quite familiar with from the circus.

"Mosey! It's Mosey!"

Kelly grinned. "She's waiting down that tunnel for you. Go on now."

Bram, with tears running down his face, gave Kelly a hug, then took off running down the tunnel. There was a faint flickering light at the end of the passage. Giant shadows danced on the wall. Bram's heart was racing.

"Mosey! Mosey!" His voice echoed in the corridor.

From the end of the tunnel came an earth-shattering trumpet. The shadow of an elephant appeared on the wall. Mosey belly-rumbled her happiness at seeing Bram.

"Mosey, girl! How I've missed you!" Bram hung on to her trunk as she brought him up to her eye. Bram kissed her cheek and tickled her ear. Mosey trumpeted in delight.

Bram barely heard Kelly telling him he'd check in on him tomorrow, and to be careful of the keepers. On into the night, Bram talked to Mosey about the trip and everything that had happened to him. He said hello to Emma, telling her what a fine daughter she had. A hug for Krono, the male elephant, who seemed to blush whenever Bram showed him any affection. And Tina, little Tina, swayed this way and that, waiting for Bram to touch her, to smother her with kisses, to tell her how beautiful she was.

Finally, Bram settled down in the hay with Mo's trunk wrapped around him. It was the first good night's sleep he'd had since leaving home.

# TWELVE

The rather large area that the elephants were being kept in had once been an engine room. Large, old engine hulks were still in place with huge, heavy steel bolts in the floor holding them down. A couple of amber-colored lights were attached to the metal walls of the room. They were wrapped in metal bars for protection and stayed on all the time.

The elephants were all chained in a row from small to large with Emma — the largest — on the end. Food was brought in every day and put just in front of them. Whenever the keepers came, Bram would hide in the straw behind the elephants until it was safe to come out. One time he had a close call when he had to sneeze.

There was no stopping it and he let out a giant snort. The keepers thought it sounded a bit unusual until Mosey came to the rescue by snorting another sneeze just like Bram's! That night Bram slept near her, talking until he fell asleep.

Bram loved the other elephants too. He would spend hours petting, watering, and feeding them, loosening their chains whenever possible.

Behind an old engine hulk, Bram found a better hiding place than the straw. He could see by the debris piled high that no one had used the space in a long time. There were some old brooms, heavy-duty water hoses, and porthole window frames, along with a rusty cabinet with a broken door that he kept his things in. He carried in some hay and a blanket Kelly gave him and settled in.

There was plenty of water from a faucet that had a huge fire hose attached to it. If Kelly couldn't get away from his job to bring food, Bram would eat with Mosey. The keepers always brought a variety of raw fruits and vegetables. Mosey was happy to share.

Across from the elephants, set way back against the wall, was a big, ancient gray cannon that was partly covered with a dusty, old army canvas. Its barrel, too long to be hidden, stuck out from underneath. Bram had seen cannons like this before in old books that showed pictures of wars from many years ago. The wheels were taller than the cannon itself!

A card tied to the gun barrel read NEW DELHI, INDIA. Bram figured it was probably a rare relic destined to be put in a museum. He could not look at it without thinking it was alive. It seemed to be thinking, waiting. Crazy thought! But sometimes, in the middle of the night, when he curled up with Mosey, he would awaken, feeling it was watching him. Heavy, thick chains wrapped around the wheels and muzzle held it firmly to the bolts in the ground. Bram felt safe knowing Mosey was there.

It was a long trip. The weeks passed slowly.

Bram listened raptly as Kelly told him of his adventures. "This time," he explained, "because we're carrying Indian cargo on board, we're going up the coast of Africa into the Bay of Bengal."

"India?" Bram said excitedly. "I read about the elephants in India. Do you think I can see any of them?"

Kelly laughed. "Not under the present circumstances — we won't be there long. This is the Indian Ocean trade route used by most vessels hauling goods. And after India — across the ocean to America."

Every morning the keepers came to feed, water, and clean the elephants. Once when Bram overslept, he came close to being found out. A keeper had come in and was going down the line of elephants with a spray to kill any flies or insects that might have been carried in on the hay. He walked completely around each elephant spraying as he went. Bram didn't have time to get to his "room." As the keeper circled each elephant, Bram kept just ahead staying low in the hay. One time he didn't move fast enough and the keeper almost stepped on him.

Bram had found a passageway that led up to a small window overlooking the upper deck. He couldn't see the ocean but he could see a lot of the activity on the deck. He saw one man sitting on ropes weaving the ends of those that had become unraveled. Others, wearing white aprons, appeared to be kitchen workers taking food on metal dishes up a spiral staircase. Bram figured it went to the captain's room or at least to his officers' quarters. Some sailors wore caps with fancy braids on them. Many appeared to be British. Others had handkerchiefs wrapped around their heads. Big, strong, unshaven men, their shirts stained with sweat, carried heavy ropes, chains, and boxes. Some of them wore no shirts at all.

A few of the sailors were Indians. Bram had seen similar people at the circus, wearing turbans and long beards. Bram rested his chin on both hands, wishing he could be out in the sun, seeing the ocean and being part of the activity. He imagined he was the captain and wore a hat with gold braids.

He had fallen asleep by the window when suddenly a hand came from behind, grabbing him by the neck. He felt himself being picked up and dragged down the staircase.

A booming voice said, "Looks like I've caught myself a stowaway!"

Bram was in pain from the pressure on his neck. Whoever held him had huge, powerful hands. But he was more concerned about what would happen to him now that he was caught!

He tried to look at the man, but his grip was too firm. At the bottom of the stairs, Bram finally got his feet under him as the man pushed him ahead.

"Please, sir, I meant no harm."

"No harm! Don't you know it's illegal to stow away on a ship?"

"But I only wanted to be with Mosey."

"Who's Mosey?"

"Mosey, my elephant."

"Your what?"

"Oh, never mind . . . you wouldn't understand."

"Well, we'll see what the captain has to say about this!"

The bright light outdoors made Bram squint as he was hurried across the deck and up a spiral staircase.

They walked through a sliding door that led to the main officers' deck. They entered a round room with maps on the wall, windows all around, and in the center a large, shiny brass wheel. A sailor was standing by it. Bram figured that he had to be the pilot.

There was a large man looking at a map on the wall. From the back Bram saw that he wore a well-pressed, dark blue suit with stripes on the sleeves and a white turban on his head. The outline of a gray beard could be seen. The hand on Bram's neck relaxed. He could feel the blood rushing back, making him feel light-headed.

The man holding him stepped forward and addressed the captain.

"Excuse me, sir, but I believe we have a stowaway."

Captain Patel turned around as the sailor saluted. Out of the corner of his eye, Bram could see the man who had held him. He was big! Maybe not as tall as String but far bigger than any man Bram had ever seen. He could understand why his head felt as though it was about to fall off.

The man's hands were unnaturally large. He wore a hat similar to the captain's, and his naval suit was immaculate. Where the captain had five stars on his collar the big man had four. His eyes were deep-set, and a strong jaw made up a man who was second to none — except the captain.

The captain looked down at Bram. "What's your name, boy?" he asked with a deep voice.

"Bram, sir, Bram Gunterstein . . . sir." The captain had piercing, cold gray eyes that seemed to burn right through Bram. "And what are you doing on my ship?"

Bram started to shake. He could barely stand on his feet. He held his own hands and finally put them under his armpits so the tremors wouldn't be noticed.

"I came with my elephant, sir."

"But all the elephants belong to the circus."

"I know, sir, but Mosey, that's her name, well we can't be apart for very long," he stammered.

"Nonsense." The captain turned to the officer. "Does he know I have the power to throw him overboard?" he asked.

"No, sir," said the officer.

The captain turned back to his map.

Bram cried, "Oh, no, sir! Please . . . sir, I didn't mean any harm. I just had to be with my elephant. I just had to. I'll do anything to make amends. Anything! I've come such a long way. After all Mosey and I been through together, please don't throw me overboard! Please!"

"Hmmmm!" said the captain. "I didn't say I *would*, I

said I *could*. I see no reason not to. However, as captain of this ship I have the power to do with you as I wish."

Bram grabbed the brass railing and hung on for all he was worth. "Please, please, sir. Let me stay."

The captain turned toward Bram. All was quiet except for Bram's heavy panting. "Give him to the cook and let him work in the galley while I consider what I should do."

"Yes, sir, captain."

As they were walking out, Bram thought he saw a bit of a smile cross the face of the man who had grabbed him.

"He's to work a twelve-hour day. Every day, you hear me?" yelled the captain.

"Yes, captain, sir."

"Now, get him out of my sight."

Bram was half dragged to the galley where he was given over to Mr. Charley, the cook. A fat man with huge arms, he wore a scarf around his neck, a band across his forehead, and a big, tall chef's hat.

For the first few weeks, Bram worked in the hot, steaming galley washing dishes, scrubbing floors, polishing the silverware, cleaning the stove, and emptying the garbage. Sometimes he felt faint and would have to hold the railing so he didn't fall. The hard work made him lose so much weight that his pants didn't fit anymore, and another kitchen worker gave him a rope to hold them up. He missed Mosey and longed to visit her and the other elephants, but it seemed like there was always somebody watching him. Besides, the ship was so large, he figured he would probably get lost.

He made a few friends. Each one had his own story of the ship, the captain, and the sea. Some were married and had wives and children at home. Others were men who loved the ocean more than anything else, and had spent their lives on it.

Bram sometimes saw Kelly walking past him on the deck or just sitting with the crew. They looked at each other, but Bram was careful not to speak to him. He didn't want to get him in any trouble.

Mr. Charley wasn't as harsh as Captain Patel, and would let Bram go up top occasionally to get a breath of fresh air. Bram's favorite pastime was to stand at the very bow of the ship where it plowed through the water causing billowing waves to form a giant wake that arced out behind them for miles. He wondered what it would be like to be the captain. He wouldn't be so nasty, that's for sure.

Bram found out that most of the crew referred to the big guy who had caught him as Hands. They said that he wasn't such a bad fellow once you got to know him.

Hands came down to see about Bram every so often. He never spoke directly to him but rather to the cook, asking if he was working out okay. The cook always gave a favorable account, saying that he was doing the work of two people and was a big help to him. Then one day, while Bram was taking a break outside on the deck, he felt a heavy hand on his shoulder. He scrunched up, remembering the time he was caught.

"Taking a break, are you?"

The voice was familiar. Hands! Panic raced through him. Would they throw him overboard?

"Please, sir, the cook said it was okay." Bram's voice was quavering.

Hands looked down at Bram. "Don't worry, everything is okay with me," he said as a smile crossed his face. "Is everything okay with you, lad?"

Bram's legs melted out from underneath him. He sat down on the edge of a hatch cover. "Yes, sir. Everything is just fine, I guess."

"You guess?"

"Well, sir. I miss my elephant."

"Why do you insist she's yours?" Hands asked, sitting down alongside Bram. For the next half hour Bram told Hands all that had happened in his life since the circus was sold, including how he had stowed away on board the ship. Hands listened intently. When Bram was through, there was a moment of silence. Finally, the cook came out, telling Bram to get back to work. Hands stood up and shook Bram's hand. As he left he said, "I'll see what I can do."

Another week passed. It was a full month since they had left port. The word was out that the captain was allowing the crew to have a full week of leave on shore when they arrived in India.

Bram was now considered a deck hand and was accepted by the crew.

He saw Kelly quite often. Bram really liked Kelly. They spoke like men, sharing their secrets and hopes for the future. The work was making Bram's body fill out with strong muscles. The sun gave him a nice bronze tan. A young man was emerging from where once stood a boy.

# THIRTEEN

It was late fall and exactly a month since Bram had started working in the galley. His free time was spent learning important things about the ship, such as how to tie knots. At night he would sit with Hands, who showed him how to navigate using a sextant, and by the stars. He explained how many ships' captains would have been lost without the ability to steer by them. Bram discovered that the dangers on a ship were many. The placement of the chain that dropped the huge anchor had to be precise or the chain could snap and the anchor would be lost.

Hands took him to the boiler room, showing him the temperature gauge and the very important steam valve that released the pressure in the engine.

Occasionally, Bram got to use Hands's long glass and

was amazed to see how close the countryside and cities along the shore of Africa appeared through the lens as they sailed north toward India. One of his great thrills was watching the great sperm whales that surfaced and "blew" their greetings. Never could he imagine any animal being bigger than Mosey, but they were at least fives times her size. On a calm night, when the ocean was tranquil, he could hear their songs intermingled with those of the dolphins.

One morning the cook told the galley staff that there was to be an inspection by the captain himself just after lunch that very day. Mr. Charley issued his orders and everybody hopped to it. Floors were mopped, and dishes, sparkling clean, were laid out in elegant fashion. All the galley staff changed into their proper uniform except for Bram. He didn't have anything but his old clothes, which by now were pretty worn. Mr. Charley put his hands on his hips, took one look at Bram, and said, "Follow me."

They disappeared into the supply area, and when they emerged a few minutes later, Bram was dressed in a full cook's uniform about two sizes too big. The pants' cuffs dragged on the floor even when rolled up, and the shirtsleeves hung below his wrists. A tightly tied rope held up his pants. The men applauded him when he appeared. Someone put a tall white hat on him that slipped down around his ears. Another stuffed paper in the rim to stop it from falling. But Bram was proud — not only of the uniform but also of having earned the respect of the crew.

"Attention!"

The whole galley crew fell into line and stood at attention, including Bram. Through the door came Captain Patel, looking his usual self — mean, arrogant, and tough. Hands was at his side, dressed in his best ship's uniform. Hands wore about half as many gold braids on his sleeves as the captain did, so it seemed to Bram that he was probably second in command. Bram was pleased to see that he was an important officer.

The captain started to walk down the aisle, checking the men's uniforms, adjusting a tie here or flicking off a bit of dust there. Every skillet was looked at, the burners checked for ashes, the floor for shoe marks. Bram stood at attention at the end of the line. The captain approached.

"Whom do we have here?" he said to Hands.

"This is the stowaway, sir."

"Hmmmm. And has he been worthy of his duties?"

"Yes, sir, all reports have been quite favorable, sir."

"Hmmmm. Very well, let's get him a proper uniform. We can't have him representing the ship in those garments, now can we?"

"No, sir. We'll take care of that right away, sir." A slight smile appeared on Hands's face.

Bram was beside himself, bursting with pride that he had been accepted by the captain himself.

Bram risked saying in a small voice, "Thank you, sir," which was barely audible.

"Hmmmm," said the captain. And started out the door. He then turned and looked directly at Bram. "By the way, there's an elephant down in the hold who has been giving everybody a good deal of trouble. Seems like she isn't sleeping all too well. Keeping everybody up, she is. See if you can assist them."

Bram's eyes brimmed with tears. He could only manage a "Yes, sir."

"Hmmmm. Yes, well, at ease men, good work, good work."

And he was gone.

Mr. Charley now gave Bram permission to see Mosey every day after work. It was late evening by the time Bram had cleared the tables, washed and dried the dishes, and mopped the floor. He pulled off his apron and headed out onto the deck, then down the stairs into the hold where the elephants were kept.

The amber lights burned dim as he approached the elephants. They were asleep. The three younger ones —

Tina, Krono, and Mosey — were all lying on their sides, sleeping. Emma stood like a guardian angel, protecting them from any harm that might come their way.

Bram shushed Emma as he went by so she wouldn't wake the others. He looked at Mosey sleeping, her huge tummy going up and down. With each exhale she made a wee whistling noise. She was snoring! He quietly took off his jacket then lay down next to her. He put the jacket under his head for a pillow and gently laid his hand on Mosey's trunk. Just before he drifted off to sleep, he thought he saw her open her eye, then close it quickly when she saw him looking at her. Bram smiled. Sleep came easily.

These were the happiest days for Bram. He worked harder and faster so he could spend more time with Mosey. The ocean was calm, the sun shining hot and bright. Dolphins raced alongside the ship, occasionally leaping from the water in graceful arcs.

As they approached the Bay of Bengal, the captain announced over the loudspeaker that they were within a few days of landing at Calcutta. But he had received information that a storm was brewing in that area. He stated that although this was not unusual, all staff and crew should prepare the ship for a storm alert.

Over the next few hours, the crew tied, bolted, and covered any and all things that were in danger of being washed away. Bram, along with the new trainer and a few of the crew, secured the hold area that housed the elephants. They checked all the tie-down chains that held the big obsolete engines to the floor, confirming that the chains weren't loose and no rust had formed. They went to the port-side hold, where all the other animals stayed — bears, lions, tigers, chimps, camels, llamas, horses. They changed their bedding so the animals would be dry and checked that the food bins were full.

Emergency lights were tested, and loose equipment was stored in boxes or lockers that were bolted to the floor. Huge, black, ominous clouds rolled in from the south and engulfed the billowy white ones. The sky darkened, the wind whipped across the deck like a wild thing, increasing its velocity by the minute. A high-pitched sound, not unlike a woman's scream, could be heard as the wind attacked the ship with a vengeance. And the ocean swells were hitting the sides of the ship with a renewed fury. From all sides the storm hammered the ship, tossing and turning it.

The storm continued throughout the night. Every so often, Bram would go up the narrow staircase to the porthole where he could see the deck. The wind howled incessantly, and each time the ship plunged into the sea, the giant waves hovered far above for a moment before crashing down on the deck. Then the ship seemed to disappear beneath the giant waves.

The dampness in the hold made the hay very slippery. Bram noticed that the elephants had to spread their legs far apart to keep their balance. He kept the area under their feet as clean and dry as possible so they would have good traction and wouldn't slip on the floor.

The storm had brought a cold front with it. Bram was freezing. He laid Mosey down, then broke open a half dozen hay bales and spread them over her body. He crawled in with her to keep warm.

A boatsman's whistle sounded over the speaker loud and clear:

"Attention! Attention! All crew members. This is your captain. Hear this! We have just received a message from the marine weather center in Calcutta. The storm has developed into a full-size hurricane with winds at its center blowing three hundred kilometers per hour! We are committed to staying on course due to our position being past the no-return mark. All personnel are to put on their life jackets and wear them at all times. I will keep you posted as to any new developments."

Early that morning, Bram was working in the galley when Hands came in to inspect this area and its equipment. He instructed the men to stow away anything that wasn't tied down. The cold storage unit was locked into position so it couldn't slide. Pots and pans were taken off the overhang and put into cabinets.

Bram caught up to him as he was leaving. "Excuse me, sir, but is there anything I can do?"

What he really wanted to know was how dangerous the storm was, but didn't want to ask, fearing that Hands would think him a coward.

"No, son, we're doing just fine." Then, as if in answer to Bram's unspoken question: "We've been through many storms and we always take precautions. This one seems to be holding its own, but one never knows how it will develop. You just keep taking care of the animals. That's a big help to us."

Hands left Bram feeling secure. Here was a giant of a man with years of experience and Bram felt lucky to have him as a friend. As for the vessel, he was told this was the ship of ships. Strong and well-built, she had traveled the seas for many years. Captain Patel, whom Bram had grown to admire and respect, was a veteran of many voyages and would keep them safe. Bram had worried about Mosey's safety, but now he could put that to rest and continue to help secure the ship. He found a passage that led to the stern hold, so it wasn't necessary to go up on deck.

He spent every minute going between the two holds, feeding and caring for the stock. A steady line of reports was coming into the radio room and then announced over the speaker system so the crew could be alerted to the size and strength of the storm.

By the second night Bram noticed that the ship was pitching more than usual. He tied a cord around a pillar and then to his leg so he wouldn't slide on the floor. The elephants, being so big and heavy, didn't slide but stayed awake all night, trying to keep their balance.

Morning. He awoke early and checked the elephants. They were a little nervous but appeared to be okay otherwise. He was curious to see what was happening on deck. Upon opening the hatch, he saw that a strong wind was whipping across the deck. The sea was a boiling mass of nature's fury. Huge waves pounded the ship's sides as she plunged deep, meeting them head on. Bram made his way to the galley. Hand over hand, he felt his way, holding on to whatever was tied down. One time he slipped as the ship plunged deep. He thought it would never right itself again.

He was exhausted by the time he reached the galley.

Water had seeped in from every crack, so he went to work mopping and scrubbing the floor. But the wind blew the rain hard and in every direction. As soon as Bram finished cleaning up, another strong wind would send more water his way.

"Forget it for now, son," said the cook. "We'll wait until the storm has let up a bit."

The galley crew gathered around the stove, keeping warm, while outside the storm continued to rage. Bram felt sorry for those who worked on deck. He hoped no one would be blown overboard.

 **FOURTEEN**

As the day wore on, the storm increased. It became impossible to walk without holding on to something. Metal pots, pans, and dishes rattled in the cabinets, which had been securely shut. A light lunch was served to those able to reach the galley. Sandwiches, hot soup, and fruit with hot coffee and yesterday's pie.

Bram was worried about Mosey. He asked permission from the cook to go to her.

"Sure, why not?" he answered. "Nothing we can do here. But you'd better be careful out there. Here, take this rope and clamp. Snap it on to the railing as you go so you won't get blown overboard."

Bram thanked him, buttoned up his jacket, and pulled

the hood down over his face. Then he strapped on his life jacket. Finally, he tied the rope to his waist, using the proper knot that the sailors had shown him. It took two men to get the door open.

The storm was hitting the ship full on. The howling wind whipped up monstrous waves that broke against the hull, sending huge geysers of water onto the deck and making it almost impossible to see.

"Are you sure you can handle it?" yelled the cook.

"I'll be okay!" Bram yelled back. Two men held the door open for him. One snapped Bram's clamp onto the outside railing and then, with their backs to the door, braced it so it wouldn't slam shut. Bram headed into the fury of the storm.

After only a few steps, he was blown off his feet and swept toward the edge of the deck. Holding on to the railing with one hand, he managed to pull himself up enough to quickly clip the clamp to the railing. As the rope took hold, it jerked him abruptly, stopping him from flying into the sea below. He pulled on the rope, hand over hand until, by sliding and scrambling, he managed to reach the railing.

Once there, he pulled himself up, then fought his way along the railing, clipping the clamp as he went. Just ahead was the hatch to the staircase that led to the hold and Mosey. The deluge beat down on him so hard he couldn't open his eyes or breathe without taking in some salt water. The wind pelted him unmercifully. Upon arriving, he pulled and pulled on the hatch but could only get it opened a few inches. The force of the wind and rain was too strong. He tried again and failed. The third time, he stuck his foot in the door to keep it open and, inch by inch, using every bit of strength he could muster, managed to squeeze through the opening. Once he was on the other side the door slammed shut.

Bram was soaked to the skin as he headed down the staircase.

"Mosey, hey, girl, are you okay?" he yelled ahead. Her loud trumpet told Bram that she was in trouble. He took the stairs three steps at a time, hit the bottom rung, raced along the corridor, and arrived in the hold to find the elephants standing in a foot of water. Anything that could float, was.

Crates, beams, boards, burlap sacks, and hay bales that had broken loose were everywhere. Tina was starting to panic. Diarrhea had set in. She was rocking back and forth, her eyes wide with fear. Bram loosened her chains so she could get closer to Krono, and they pressed together for support. Once she could touch him, she calmed down. Mosey was standing still. She seemed to be checking everything out, getting ready for whatever came her way. Bram gave her trunk a hug, then went to each elephant, running his hands over them, assuring them that everything was all right.

"It's okay everybody, just relax now and everything will be fine," he said, wishing he could believe his own words.

Bram's presence gave the elephants the security they needed. One by one they settled down, waiting to see what was going to happen to change their uncomfortable surroundings.

Bram felt as if somebody was looking at him from behind. He glanced over his shoulder and saw that the canvas cover that had been lying over the cannon had been dislodged and swept away by the water. The long muzzle of the cannon pointed straight at Mosey. Its wheels were now halfway submerged in water. As Bram looked, the cannon moved! The water was pushing against it, and each time the ship lurched, the cannon rolled a bit farther and the chains holding it were pulled tighter. The water had weakened them, and Bram could see they were wearing thin. He was terrified that it would get loose.

What am I worried about? he asked himself. It's only a piece of metal. It can't think, can it? But if it were to break loose, there would be no way to control it. It must weigh as much as Emma, he figured.

Bram heard someone sloshing through the water. It was Hands.

"Hands," he said, "what's the latest news about the storm? Are we going to be okay? The water's rising, and the elephants are getting scared."

Hands sat down on a heavy crate that hadn't floated free. "Bram, come here, boy."

Bram heard the distress in his voice. He jumped up on the crate to sit with him and tried to be brave.

"Hands, is the ship going to sink? But isn't it too big? I mean, how could it?" Bram's mind was racing, his questions toppling out on top of one another.

"Bram, I want you to listen to me." The seriousness in Hands's voice shocked Bram. His eyes kept shifting to the top deck. "The storm is getting worse, much worse than we thought. We sent out a distress call, but there is no one close enough to help."

"What are we going to do?" asked Bram, tears starting to well up in his eyes at the thought of losing Mosey and the others.

Hands thought for a moment. "We have to go up top."

"How do we get Mosey and the others up there?"

Hands slowly shook his head and looked into Bram's face. "We don't, son."

"But we have to! We can't just leave them here! Why, Mosey would be frightened, and —"

"Bram, listen to me!" He grabbed his arms tight and shook him. "We have to go up, now!"

"I can't leave them. No! I can't!" Bram pulled away from Hands.

"I'm not saying that we won't make it," said Hands, "but if there is a problem, we must be on the deck to survive."

All of a sudden, the ship rolled and the crate they sat on began to slide. Tina's legs went out from under her, and she crashed to the floor. She trumpeted her distress.

Karno and Emma were now in a state of sheer panic, slipping on the wet floor, bumping into the pillars and trumpeting.

Hands lifted Bram off the crate as it slid into the wall. Three loud honks of the ship's alarm blared into the hold. A red light started flashing. Bram ran to help Tina regain her balance.

Hands yelled, "Bram! They need me up above. Come on, now!"

"You go, Hands, I'll be okay. Please, you've been a good friend. You better go now though. You're needed on deck."

Hands was in a state of frenzy. Bram could see that he didn't want to leave them, but he knew he had to respond to the state of emergency. That was his job. Hands reluctantly made a decision.

"Take care, Bram, take care. May God be with you." His voice trailed off, lost in the noise of the blaring horn and howling wind.

## FIFTEEN

The cold ocean water was rising faster now. Fortunately the floor of the ship warmed it some, but it still caused the elephants to shiver. Bram went to Mosey. The water was lapping at her knees. She was swaying back and forth holding on, facing her fear of the unknown. She stopped her swaying the minute Bram touched her, content that now everything would be all right. The others sensed her calmness and responded as well. Bram went to each elephant, speaking to them, trying to calm them the best he could. He spoke of Curpo and Gertie and all his other friends. Mosey, hearing their names, belly-rumbled.

Bram wrestled with the idea of undoing their chains. Without them, his control would be limited, yet they would have freedom to move about. Then all of a sudden everything stopped. All was quiet. The ship's pitching and rolling subsided. The sloshing water in the hold came to a standstill and remained calm.

The elephants stopped their swaying, the red light shut off as well as the horn. A quiet came over the vessel.

"It's over!" yelled Bram. "It's over! The storm is gone!"

Mosey saw Bram's enthusiasm and trumpeted. The other elephants responded with their thunderous bellows. Bram hugged them all. He saw a light coming down the corridor toward them. It was Kelly and a few of his men.

"Kelly, it's over. The storm is gone."

He gave Kelly a big hug, jumping around like a puppy. Then he noticed that Kelly didn't seem to share his enthusiasm. "No, Bram, it's not over."

"But it's gone," Bram said. "There's no more storm. Everything is back to normal."

"We're in the eye," Kelly said.

"Whose eye?" Bram was completely confused. Kelly became sympathetic when he saw the innocence in Bram's questioning face.

"Bram," Kelly said, "all hurricanes have an eye, a center. This is where all the energy of the storm comes from. When you reach the center, everything is quiet and peaceful. The sky clears, the sea becomes calm. Until . . .

you move through it. Until you reach the other side. Then it starts all over again, only this time it's going in the opposite direction. You know, Bram, what it didn't do the first time" — his voice trembled — "it'll do now."

"You mean it's coming back?"

"'Fraid so. We have just a short time to prepare for it."

"Prepare how? There is no way to prepare for it. It's too big, too monstrous."

Kelly took Bram's hand. "Bram, you have to come topside. If things go bad, at least you'll have a chance but down here . . . none."

Bram sobered up. "So, it's coming back. Well, let's prepare, in this little time we have before it hits. Thanks, Kelly, you better get back up. I am sure there are a lot of people that need help above."

"Bram, you're coming, aren't you?"

"Yeah, I'll be right behind you."

"Okay, but make it quick. See ya, Bram."

"See ya, Kelly. And thanks."

Bram figured he would die. The elephants too. They had relaxed somewhat and were munching on hay. It's better that they don't know, he thought. He pulled a bale of wet hay over to Mosey and sat on it. She played with his hair, running the tip of her trunk through it. Bram closed his eyes and prayed. He tried very hard to be able to see God, to speak to him personally, and ask for his help. Bram spoke out loud.

"I know you must be very busy up there, but if you have time to help Mosey and the other elephants, I would surely appreciate it. Maybe animals don't get the same treatment as humans. If they don't, could you at least have Mosey stay in the humans' heaven, with me, if that's okay?" Bram thought a moment. "But well, everybody on the ship needs your help and . . . anyway, do what you can."

Bram thought of his father in the coffin. He didn't understand death then and surely didn't now. He was scared.

Mama is sure going to be mad if I die, he thought.

But the most important thing now was to be with Mosey. He would worry about dying later. One thing he had to be careful with was Mosey reading his mind. She was so sensitive to his feelings and he didn't want to alarm her.

The ship shifted a little. He waited. It shifted again, harder. Bram's heart began to race. The water in the hold started to move, sloshing up one side of the bulkhead and then the other. The elephants froze in their positions. They knew. It was back.

Within minutes the hurricane was at its full fury. The

ship was rolling and plunging into the waves, the wind howling so hard he could hear it through the walls.

The cannon was rocking hard, pushing and pulling against the rusty weather-worn chains, with each toss of the ship. Then, one of the large chains snapped! The cannon moved forward.

Bram decided to let the elephants loose so they could get out of its way if it rolled in their direction. He started with Tina. Using a pair of pliers, he unscrewed the swivel and the chain fell away from her leg. He repeated this with Krono and Emma.

Four foot high waves, caused by the rocking of the ship, battered them. Huge wooden beams broke loose and floated dangerously close, ramming the steel pillars that supported the ceiling and walls. Bram waded over to Mosey.

"Okay, girl, try to raise your foot so I can get that chain off." She tried but the water was too high. "It's okay, I can do it underwater."

Putting his hands under the water, Bram felt for the swivel. Just as he found it, a floating plank hit him in the back, knocking him face first into the water. Bram panicked. The force had knocked the pliers from his hand. He searched and searched but couldn't find them. A loud popping sound came from behind him. His eyes were still blurry from water. He wiped them quickly only to see that the cannon had broken free and was rolling toward Mosey!

Bram knew if it hit her it could kill her. Again, he frantically searched for the pliers. Nothing. The cannon had picked up speed and was only a few yards from her when the ship shifted and the cannon rolled back to its lair. Bram was terrified that the next time the cannon would reach Mosey. He held his breath and went under.

The water was too dirty to see anything. Only by feel would he have a chance to find the pliers. Underwater, he felt the ship shift again. He knew that the cannon would soon be coming at Mosey. Then, he felt them! Grasping them hard, he surfaced to see that the cannon was on its way. Bram scrambled to get the chain off. But it was too late.

A large beam blocked the cannon's forward motion for an instant. Bram realized the only way was for Mosey to break the chain!

"Move up! Mosey. Move up, now!" he yelled.

The cannon had broken loose from the floating beam and was on its way!

"Move, Mosey! Now, girl! Pull. Pull! Now!"

Mosey strained with all her strength. The chain broke just in time. The cannon missed her by a few inches. The elephants could at least move out of the way now. The cannon, with nothing to stop it, traveled all the way across the hold and pounded into the side of the ship, knocking a huge dent in it. With each roll of the ship, it hit the same spot until the dent in the steel-plated wall began to show serious damage.

The elephants were in a state of sheer panic. Every time the cannon made its run, they scrambled to get out of the way. Sometimes, it missed its mark and crashed into a pillar, but most of the time it hit the same wall.

The hold of the ship was a mad, horrible, sight. Giant waves picked up debris, slamming it against the wall. The huge beams continued their destructive rampage, breaking gas and electric valves. Sparks flew from the water. The flashing red light was still flashing, even though it was now under water.

The battering of the hull continued. Then, Bram saw it. The cannon had broken through! A small hole allowed the water to come in. Again the cannon made its run, hitting the wall hard. Bram watched as the hole grew bigger and bigger. With an earth-shattering ripping noise, the whole side of the wall cracked open. A huge wave from the ocean exploded into the chamber!

Bram and the elephants were lost in an underwater ballet of drifting bodies, all confused, not knowing which way was up or down. Bram felt his body being tossed around like a cork. Pulled and pushed, he struggled for air, but there was none. Inside his mind, he screamed for Mosey. He felt the pain of losing her even in this terrifying moment.

All of a sudden Bram realized he was on the surface of the ocean, being carried from one giant wave to another. The waves were as high as the ship had been. He coughed, retching until his stomach ached, sputtering out the salt water he had swallowed. The sea and sky seemed to meet; he couldn't tell which way was up. He was thrashing, trying to catch his breath. Lightning cracked, and for a moment, Bram regained his balance. He saw, in the momentary flash of light, the immensity of the ocean. As far as he could see, there was nothing, no one. And though the water was warm, he couldn't stop shivering.

Was it possible that the great ship had sunk? And that everything and everybody had gone down with it?

Then he saw a large object coming toward him, traveling quickly. A wooden beam rode the waves just as he did. He tried to swim to it, but it was just out of reach and disappeared into the darkness. Other pieces of wreckage from the ship floated by. It seemed impossible. That gigantic ship! Sinking.

His mind wouldn't let him think of Mosey or the other elephants. It was too much, too hard, the pain would be impossible. Some pieces of crates, boxes, and timber floated by, too small to grab onto. He floated on his back, exhausted from the struggle, letting his arms lay still in the water.

Then he heard a voice carried to him by the wind from far away. People!

The sky lit up with a lightning flash. Could it be there were people like him floating in the stormy waters? He yelled, "Hello out there! Anybody hear me?" He waited. Again, "Hellooooo!"

Nothing. A small chunk of wood drifted by. He grabbed and hung on to it so he wouldn't have to tread water. He heard the voices again from afar.

He yelled again. "Helloooo!"

This time they answered. "Hellooo! Over here!"

Bram turned in a circle. As the lightning flashed, he saw a group of people hanging on to one another. The waves were carrying them in his direction. Closer and closer they came. For a moment it looked as if he might miss them, so he left the board and swam fast, hoping to reach them before they were out of sight. A few stretched out their hands to help until he was brought into their circle.

He recognized some of the deck hands and the boiler crew. The stronger swimmers supported the weaker, while others floated on their backs to conserve strength. Bram could see it was only a matter of time before their exhaustion would take them under. Everybody was talking at once.

"Have you seen any other survivors?"

"No. None."

"Any part of the wreckage?"

"Just a few pieces."

"What about the captain?"

"No. Nothing."

Bram was saddened to think of Captain Patel, Kelly, Hands, and all the crew and animals that might have gone down with the ship.

He asked if anybody had seen an elephant. Everybody shook their heads no. Some knew how close Bram had been to Mosey.

"No, nothing. Haven't seen any of them," said one of the deckhands.

"What are we going to do?" asked another.

"How far are we from land?"

"No one knows."

A couple of the sailors were injured. Others were trying to keep them afloat.

"We're all going to die, I just know it," spoke a wounded sailor.

Bram looked around. He saw gray-white faces, exhausted men, some with cuts on their faces and arms. "Let's not give up," he said. "I'm sure there will be a boat to pick us up."

"Yeah, but when?" asked another.

"How long can we last in this water?"

No one answered.

They heard shouting from close by. A few more stragglers drifted their way. Some were too far to reach, others they grabbed with outstretched hands. It was getting too dark to see who was in the circle, but Bram had counted thirty-four people hanging on to one another.

The waves had subsided a bit but they were still huge and forbidding.

During the next few hours the sky darkened. The day was over. People came and went. Those who could, hung on, those who couldn't, just floated away — too weak to care, their injuries too bad for them to last.

Bram was half asleep when he felt a hand on his neck. Not just a hand but a big hand. He jolted awake — could it be?

"Hands, is that you?"

"It is, my friend, it is."

Bram was so excited he practically jumped out of the water to throw his arms around Hands. They spoke of many things. The ship. The crew. Mosey.

"I miss her so much."

"I know, son, she was a great elephant. Maybe someday another will come."

"There will never be another like her."

Bram felt a knot in his stomach as he had when his father had died. It hurt so much. He changed the subject. "Would the captain really have thrown me overboard that first day?"

"Well," Hands said, with a small chuckle, "you never know."

The storm had gone but the waves continued to carry them high to their crests and then plunge them down to where they were in danger of being pulled apart in the curls.

Bram had tied himself to Hands so he could float and rest awhile without drifting away. He slipped in and out of sleep, reliving the horror of what had happened. When he thought of the elephants, he cried, his tears joining the sea.

In his dream, he could hear Mosey trumpeting. He moved a bit closer to Hands. The dream was gone. But the trumpeting stayed.

"Hands, did you hear that?"

It came again.

"Hands, did you hear that?"

"What?"

"Listen."

Again the sound.

"It's an elephant!"

"No. Impossible," said Hands.

Again, closer now.

"It's Mosey! Hands! It's Mosey!"

Bram climbed on top of Hands, practically pushing him under the water, in hopes of seeing farther. Way off, the sound of an elephant could be heard. Trumpeting.

"Oh! My God!" Bram was in a panic. "Mosey!" he yelled.

Over the giant waves the trumpeting became louder.

"There, over there! Look!" said one of the sailors.

Coming in their direction was a large, dark object floating on the massive waves.

"It's Mosey! Hands, I know it! It's Mosey!"

As the object came closer, Hands could see that it was an elephant, but he couldn't make out which one.

Bram cried, "We're going to miss her! She's too far away!"

# SIXTEEN

Bram started to swim toward the elephant. He felt the rope that was tied to Hands tighten. Bram scrambled to take off the rope.

Hands grabbed him. "No! Bram, wait! Don't do that. If you miss her, you'll be lost." Hands yelled at the others, "Listen, everybody. Open the circle. Everybody stretch out, form a line. Hold hands." Hands took the rope off of Bram, who reached out as Mosey went by. Mosey grabbed his arm with her trunk. The line closed around her.

"Mosey!" he screamed. "It is you!"

And it was. She belly-rumbled, shaking her head, trumpeting and blasting the air with her excitement at finding Bram, who was climbing all over her, hugging every part of her body.

"Elephants float really well. She's our island," Bram said proudly.

"Let's put only the sick or injured on her back. The rest should hang on to her sides. We don't want to tire her out," offered Hands.

"But we have to keep her trunk up or she could drown," added Bram.

Hands organized a schedule where five men would tread water in front of Mosey, so she could stretch her trunk across their shoulders. Every half hour they were replaced by five others. At first she thought it good fun and would wiggle and tickle their faces. Bram swam under Mosey and came up in his favorite place, under her chin. The five men treading water held her trunk up, so there was plenty of space for Bram, where he curled up, as if it were his own private room. He told her all about the things he had experienced.

Hands stationed himself near Bram, keeping an eye on him.

"How do you think she got out?" Bram asked Hands.

"Probably the same way you did — through the break in the wall. It was the only thing big enough. I think the ocean sucked everything out of that hole. It's just that some survived."

The days and nights came and went. There was no sign of a ship that could rescue them.

"Thank God we're in the Indian Ocean," said Hands. "It's subtropical. The water's fairly warm. If this had happened in the Atlantic, we wouldn't have lasted an hour."

The storm had moved out of the area. The sea was silent. A thick fog lay on the water. It had slowly rolled in during the night. Only the occasional splash of one of the men adjusting himself could be heard.

Bram noticed that Mosey was starting to tire. Some of the men supporting her trunk would fall asleep and let it hang in the water.

"Let's make a raft," said Bram. "For Mosey's trunk."

"You must be kidding," answered another. "We can barely keep ourselves afloat."

"And besides, what the hell are we going to build a raft with? Seaweed?"

"We had better keep her trunk up," Hands said. "If anything happens to her, we're all doomed. We can use anything that comes by — as long as it's floating."

And so they did. Whenever a piece of wood floated by, they would add it to their collection. Finally Hands had enough pieces to crisscross and make a small raft for

Mosey to rest her trunk on. This enabled her to sleep and rest a bit. It also allowed the men who were supporting her trunk to save their strength. Though the men were exhausted, they saw the value of their work. Mosey could now relax her trunk and save her energy, which gave them a better chance of survival.

Bram noticed that Mosey was swimming. Her feet were constantly moving. He went beneath the surface of the water to hold her feet so they didn't move, showing her it wasn't necessary. All she had to do was float. She needed to conserve her energy.

The sea had become calm. Small shallow waves lapped against Mosey's side as if on a shore on some distant island. Everyone's hunger, thirst, and injuries were taking their toll. At night, some chose to just slip away into watery graves. Others held out, hoping that they would be rescued.

Bram counted only twenty-seven people clinging to Mosey. Everyone was thirsty. One man joked about all this water and nothing to drink. They knew that drinking salt water would make them very sick. Occasionally, birds would fly by, hovering above the strange group, then move on. Sometimes during daylight hours Bram would stand on Mosey's back, hoping to see some sign of a boat or land, but nothing appeared. Most of the time a thick fog rolled in at night and would stay for the remainder of the day.

"How will they ever find us in this?" one of the men from the galley asked.

For three days they survived together in a haunting environment of water, air, and fog. Bram would sit and talk into Mosey's ear about the days at the farm, about his father, the circus, the life he had led. He spoke of Gertie and Curpo. It all seemed so very long ago.

On the evening of the third day, a fog horn suddenly blared in the distance. Again the sound. Slowly the weakened crew members realized a boat was coming — they would be saved after all.

"Someone is coming! Someone is coming!"

"Praise the Lord, thank you, thank you."

Then, out of the fog, a small boat, not much bigger than Mosey, appeared. As the horn sounded, a bell rang. It drifted nearer.

"Hello out there!" a pleasant voice cried.

"We're here! Over here!" yelled Hands.

The boat came closer.

"Cut the engines."

"Aye aye, sir," was the response.

The boat slowed until it rested against the side of Mosey. The people, some crying, some too sick to show their emotion, scrambled into it. Hands assisted those who were too weak to make it. A man with a thick dark beard and wearing a red turban greeted the group.

"I am the captain of this small, miserable boat and we welcome you."

Hands had introduced himself after helping the others. When all were loaded, Hands called to Bram.

"We have to go, son."

"We're never going to get Mosey on the boat, Hands, are we?" Bram's voice was shaking.

"No, it's too small a boat, but they will send another boat for her, I am sure. Now, please, let's go."

"No, I can't."

Hands turned to speak to the captain. "There must be something we can do."

A number of the survivors were also protesting. "She saved our lives."

"You can't just leave her!"

"We owe her!"

"We've been to hell and back!"

The captain became upset and apologetic. He saw the suffering in their eyes. "I am very sorry," he pleaded, "but my boat is just a humble little vessel."

Hands asked, "Can't we tow her?"

"I am afraid not. We would never make it back to

shore. It would jeopardize everyone. Why, she is as big as my boat!"

"We can't just do nothing!" someone cried.

"This isn't fair!"

The captain raised his hands to quiet them. "Look, when we return to port, I will personally see to it that they send a larger boat. I promise." The captain pulled Hands aside and spoke in a whisper. "Please, sir, a moment. There is another storm brewing and we must leave now. I think it is highly unlikely that she will be rescued."

When Hands looked back, Bram had drifted with Mosey away from the boat. They were moving farther and farther away into the fog.

"Bram, where are you going? Come back!"

"You go on, Hands, they'll need you. I'll manage. Maybe a bigger boat will come. I can't leave her, I just can't." Bram was in tears. They had come so close to being rescued and now this.

Other people frantically called out for Bram to return to the boat, but their voices were lost in the silence of the fog.

"Good-bye, Hands, tell my family I love them." Bram's voice trailed off in the void.

"Bram, come back!" yelled Hands. His voice reflected the tears in his eyes, "Come back, my friend, come back."

Like a blanket, the fog slowly enveloped Mosey.

# SEVENTEEN

Bram heard the foghorn of the little boat long after it had left. The sea was quiet. The thick fog had settled on the water like the cream his mother used to make. Any movement caused it to float around for a while until it settled once again on the waters surface.

Bram had put the wooden raft well under Mosey's trunk so she could rest more easily. He crawled down underneath her chin into his private place. Here there was no fog to remind him of where he was. He talked to her, falling asleep every so often. Mosey, too, drifted in and out of sleep. They were both in need of rest, food, and water. Sometimes Bram's head would go beneath the water and he would take a gulp, coming up coughing and wheezing. Other times, Mosey's trunk would slip into the water, waking her in time to pull it out before inhaling.

Another day passed. Bram felt he was in a bubble of fog he would never get out of.

The sea turned rough again. Bram thought he had heard the man on the ship talking about another storm coming. Mosey was hardly moving at all. She was now depending on the wooden raft to support her head as well as her trunk, and most of the time her head was in the water. She was fighting for air.

Bram could no longer hold on to Mosey. He had lost all strength in his legs and arms. The salt water had burned his eyes. They were swollen shut. Only the confines of his private room kept him from floating away. He spoke to Mosey, but his words were barely audible. "Mosey . . . sorry about this. Thought . . . we'd make it to New York. You would've been . . . a great star." His mind drifted, and he shook his head to stay awake. "Wonder what Mama'll do when she hears. . . . Hope she'll forgive." He reached out and touched Mosey's cheek, but his hand had turned numb. All feeling was gone.

His thoughts turned to Gertie. The slightest smile crossed his face. "We were going to have children. And travel . . . together."

It was time to go. Bram didn't want to die before Mosey. He couldn't bear the thought of her being alone were he to die first. Bram crawled up to her eye. He patted the soft skin around it.

"Mosey . . . time to go. Can't wait anymore. Sea's getting rough . . . will take us soon. Better we do it than the ocean."

Mosey looked at Bram, her eye following his every move. This was the boy she cherished. All her trust and love was in her gaze. She seemed to know what had to be done.

Bram gathered his last ounce of strength to give her instructions. His voice was calm, he was ready. "I'm going to pull the raft away and put my arm in your mouth. Hold my arm. Don't let go. No matter what — don't let go." He took a deep breath. "We'll be together always. No one . . . can ever . . . hurt us."

Bram wiped the tears from his eyes. He ran his finger over the smooth skin around her eye and laid his cheek against hers. "I love you, Mosey."

Bram got under her and gently raised her head. Then, on his word, she relaxed her huge jaw allowing Bram to put his arm in. "Okay, now hold tight." Bram could feel her gently press and hold his arm. "Now I'm going to slip this board out from under your trunk and when I do, you just keep thinking of the circus, the flower fields, Curpo, and all your friends."

Tears flowed freely down Bram's cheeks as he gently pushed the little wooden raft away. It floated into the fog as Mosey and Bram sunk beneath the water, down, down into a warm, fluid world. Mosey didn't fight it. Her huge head slowly sank with Bram's arm locked in her mouth. She instinctively knew they were at the end of their journey. Bram's thoughts were of his life back home, his mother and father, of playing with Gertie and Curpo and Mosey in the flower fields. For a moment all he felt was the bubbles. The agonizing wash of the sea was gone and peace and quiet descended on him. He was slowly letting his breath out when he heard a noise. A distinct sound like the vibration of a motor. It was getting louder!

Something was happening. Bram wrenched and twisted, trying to get free. He wanted to see what it was, but Mosey's lock on his arm was firm. He tried to get loose but couldn't. He pounded on her cheek but it was futile, and they sank deeper. Then, a huge ear-splitting bang rocked the water. It was so enormous that Mosey burst to the surface, carrying Bram with her. A dozen men were in the water. Some were supporting Mosey's head and trunk while others swam under her, fastening a huge canvas sling beneath her belly. Massive ropes were encircling her. Mosey relaxed her grip on Bram's arm. Bram felt he was sliding down, down a watery tunnel into a chasm of liquid space. He heard voices from far away calling him.

"Bram! Bram!"

He felt his body being lifted. Slowly he opened his swollen eyes. Water blurred his vision, but it cleared enough so that he could make out a familiar face.

"Hands?" he whispered.

"Hang on, Bram, I've got ya. Stay with me now. Everything's gonna be okay."

He carefully lifted Bram to waiting arms on the deck of the large Indian ferryboat, then hoisted himself up, and followed Bram to a waiting cot where he was quickly covered with blankets. Hands massaged Bram's arms and legs. The color was slowly returning to his face.

"Come on, fella — you got an elephant to take care of."

Men in the water were working feverishly, holding Mosey's head above water as a giant crane slowly raised her from the ocean and carefully lowered her onto the deck of the boat. With a signal from the captain, the engines started up, and the boat cut its way through the fog.

Water poured from Mosey's mouth and trunk, but she was breathing.

Bram slowly came to. He upchucked a mouthful of water, coughing and sputtering; then, as his vision cleared, he looked up and weakly smiled at Hands.

"Hands, Hands," he whispered, and gave him a hug.

"Hey, sailor, welcome back." Hands smiled. Cheers went up from the crew all around as Bram sat up, coughing. He heard a weak belly rumble coming from behind him. He turned to see Mosey lying flat on the deck. She was covered in blankets and ten men were busy drying her off and caring for her.

He tried to stand but fell back into Hands's arms. Hands picked Bram up and carried him across the deck to her.

"Mosey!" said Bram, barely audible as Hands lowered him down to her.

Too exhausted to rise, Mosey followed him with her eye. Bram whispered into her ear. "I love you, Mosey."

Mosey's belly rumble was heard throughout the boat.

# EPILOGUE

For a ferryboat to go out into the open sea was unheard of. It was thought it could not survive due to its low deck, and with a storm coming within hours, the rescue was daring and heartrending.

Bram and Mosey were taken to Calcutta, India, where they recovered from their ordeal. Here they were befriended by a maharajah who allowed Bram and Mosey to stay at his palace and elephantarium. Bram lived a spiritual life at the palace, where he met and "experienced" Atoul, the famous white elephant.

When word came that Mr. North, the new circus owner, had discovered their whereabouts and was about to reclaim Mosey as his own, Bram was forced to leave. Their journey took him on many adventures, including thwarting an attempt by ruthless bandits to steal Mosey, living in a teak forest village, being caught up in a war between Ethiopia and India, and, eventually, joining the circus, where he performed at the world-famous Madison Square Garden in New York.

Bram's mother lived a peaceful life at the farm and passed away before Bram could bring her to America.

Years later, Curpo brought Gertie to the United States, and she and Bram were married. They lived happily together with Mosey at the circus.

All those who knew Mosey and those who watched her perform agreed: she truly was the greatest elephant that ever lived!